D1554479

Moody & The Ghost
Dead Ahead

KIM HORNSBY

PRESS
SEATTLE * MAUI

Acknowledgements

There are always scads of people to thank for helping make a book a reality. Luckily, I don't have all those editors, agents and publishing people to list because I'm an Indie Author. My staff are my husband, who supplies meals and support, and my dogs who supply entertainment and foot warming on cold days. There are always various sub-contractors who don't do any of that care-giving stuff and actually get paid.

My grandmother, Ida Hornsby, believed in ghosts and I was raised believing it's not only a possibility but a probability. Thank you, Nana, for being ahead of your time.

I have a wonderful group of writer friends who inspire me to be as wonderful as they believe I am. Thank you for cheering me on, tirelessly.

To JD DeWitt, my Literary Manager, who encourages me and inspires me to be her best book to film client. I am humbly appreciative of your dedication to my writing. When I don't final in a screenwriting contest, I only need to remember I have JD on my side.

To Robin McLain, whose business card I keep in my wallet to remind me that I'm a big deal and attracted the attention of a movie producer with keen vision.

To my group of super fan/beta readers who I affectionately call Kim's Krowd, who gave me direction and advice on this one. You know exactly who you are, and I won't list your names because you review, and bots will take your reviews off if they connect us.

And to Ann Charles who inspires me and has guided me in Indie Authorship.

To Steve Novak at Novak Illustrations who designs amazing covers for next to nothing.

To be allowed the luxury and privilege of writing books, I need my immediate family on board with this writing thing. Expectations must be set very low for meals, laundry, even conversation. It's selfish of me, but I'd be a crazy woman without writing. To my husband, Roland, who hears "shh" more times than any husband should, to Jack whose texts are grammatically perfect, something I'm so frickin' proud of, and to Ila who has taught me to have a tougher heart or I'm going to crumble. I'm sorry I stopped playing Super-Mom a little early and became Writer-Mom. I hope it worked to your advantage to not have me peering over your shoulders constantly.

Dedication

To my dear friend, Catharina, who suggested I write something funny.

We cannot direct the wind, but we can adjust the sails.

~ *Bertha Calloway*

CHAPTER 1

Five months ago, I was perfectly capable of more than descending a staircase on my own. I often took two stairs at a time.

These days, I must be helped down stairs by my younger cousin, Eve. Being dependent on someone else 24/7 was on my This Totally Sucks list, along with having someone buy my groceries and lead me to a car I can no longer drive. And, although this next one doesn't keep me from functioning, I have a large cut on my face that's "healing nicely," according to the plastic surgeon. The wound I originally named "Frankenscar" runs from my cheek to my chin and is responsible for introducing me to scads of doctors and nurses at Seattle's Swedish Hospital in the last few months.

There have been many adjustments since the accident, not the least of which was the loss of my soul mate, Harrison Moody. But, I can't talk about Harry. Not yet. I'm trying to concentrate on the positive, as suggested by everyone who knows me. Including the woman helping me down the stairs, Evelyn Xio Primrose, a woman with whom I used to share that last name until I married Harry last year. Then I became a Moody.

My name is Bryndle Moody and I have a YouTube show called Moody Paranormal Investigations. Ghosts are my specialty. They love me. In the biz, I'm known as a medium, but I like the more badass term

Ghost Hunter, even though my small team of investigators hunts to help ghosts, not annihilate them. I'm a bit of a celebrity in paranormal circles. At least I used to be.

I'm known to my YouTube followers as Moody, which is appropriate as I attempt to adjust not only to being a young widow but being as blind as a bat. This expression, I have recently found out, isn't accurate. Bats are not blind. I looked it up online with the help of my vocal software that translates screen to audio.

As I walked to the car, on Eve's arm, I thought how this day was getting stranger every hour. First, I woke to my mother, Rachel Primrose, calling my cell phone to say her neighbor and friend, Mrs. Giovanni, had died mysteriously.

"I watched the ambulance take her away just now. Horrible. She was such a good neighbor."

My mother wanted me to come over to do a reading. "Why not let the police handle it?" I asked, knowing better than to engage with her, but I was fuzzy from sleep and temporarily forgot her history of being a dangerously aggressive budinski.

"They think she died in her sleep, but that daughter of hers . . ."

"I'll call you later," I said, ending the call. My mother and I have a complicated relationship. That doesn't stop her from calling me three times a day. Or me from hanging up on her at least twice. We have a strange dependency on each other.

Then, while walking from the houseboat to my car an hour ago, a crow landed on my shoulder. Eve screamed when she saw the big thing alight on me, but I happen to love crows. At the age of eight, I once befriended one who could say "Shut the god-damned door." It flew away after a few days of hanging around my uncle Ogden's house, where we lived temporarily. They are so incredibly smart. If my telepathy wasn't dead-in-the-water right now, I might have known why this morning's crow came to me. I'd often had fleeting glimpses into my dog Hodor's mind. But, I didn't get anything from the crow except that it thought I was its private launch pad. I just stood very still, enjoying the moment with the weight of a large bird on my right shoulder until Eve shooed it away.

"Scram," she said, after her little yelp to see a large black bird on me.

Eve is very protective, sometimes taking her job as my assistant a little too seriously. I later wished she'd gotten a photo of the crow sitting on the shoulder of my favorite pleather jacket. I choose not to wear real leather, but I don't judge. I eat hamburgers, so go figure.

With social media such a big deal now, and me a business owner, I was constantly telling either Eve or my tech guy, Carlos, to take a picture for our Snapchat, Facebook, Instagram, or Twitter accounts. Today was no different except I was too thrilled to have the weight of a crow on my shoulder that I didn't dare say anything. You could say Moody Investigations is as big on social media as we are on ghosts. YouTube is our livelihood, our bread and butter.

On the drive to Seattle's downtown, I wondered if the crow was Mrs. Giovanni, then realized that was not possible. It was a strange thought, even for someone who believed in some pretty wacky stuff.

The next unusual event occurred when we arrived at the lawyer's office, were seated, and were told that I'd inherited a house from someone I had no recollection of ever meeting. I'd previously been informed there was something left to me in this woman's will, and I'd thought maybe as a fan of the show, she'd left me a weird statue or a favorite black cape. But the woman, Belinda McMahon, had left me a house. On a piece of property. In Oregon, which was the next state over. I didn't know yet if the house was a dilapidated shed on a sliver of swampland, but the fact that someone wanted me to have her house was both touching and mysterious. Unless the house came with a curse.

Unfortunately, the lawyer, a man named Sheldon Rinkle (who Eve had secretly renamed Seldom Wrinkled), knew nothing about the structure, only that I was the recipient of the house.

The deal was that if I accepted the house, I couldn't sell it for five years. I immediately wondered how many years of upkeep I'd have to contribute to warrant inheriting real estate. And how much I'd need to spend on taxes. Then, Mr. Wrinkled told me five years' worth of taxes and repairs had been factored into an account his office was paid to manage.

Very mysterious.

Walking across the parking garage, I suggested Eve and I both pretend to be blind when we saw a car coming. "Keep your eyes open a little to tell me if they look horrified," I said. But no cars approached, and I didn't think Eve was totally on board with my little joke. Knowing her, she'd think it was unsafe for her even to partially close her eyes in a parking lot.

Eve and I arrived at my car, a 1961 Austin Healey Bugeye Sprite, I'd named Austin, years ago. I used to drive that little wonder all over Seattle. Until the accident. Of course, now I didn't drive. I couldn't even find Austin in a garage without help. Even though he was bright red.

I fastened my probably inadequate lap belt, which only kept me from flying out of the car in an accident, not hitting my head on the dashboard, and waited for my cousin to get into the driver's seat. I fingered the belt, thinking about another car, one that was now in a scrap heap somewhere, crushed on the driver's side. Whenever my mind took me to that scary day, I pushed the memory aside, like a dreaded house chore to be tackled later.

"I'm gobsmacked that someone I do not know, would leave me a house," I said.

This new turn of events was all very strange and left me feeling like I was in a dream. But then, the whole last five months had felt like a dream. The difference was being left a house was a good kind of dream, especially if the house was paid for.

According to the attorney, the property was near a small town named Smuggler's Cove on the Oregon coast. That sounded charming. And slightly illegal. I was intrigued, because I'm drawn to bad things--always have been. Harry was the exception. My therapist had approved of my choice in men when I fell for the slightly nerdy-looking but steadfast and hugely funny Harry Moody.

As Austin roared to life, I asked Eve what she thought. "Did the attorney seem legit?" It wasn't necessary to turn my head to look at my cousin. I couldn't see, true, but I knew what she looked like. She'd be wearing ripped jeans, a Hello Kitty jacket and skull jewelry. Or something similar. Her long black hair would be in high pigtails or in a bun planted on the very top of her head maybe held together with chopsticks. She might even have the ends of her hair bleached with pink tints. Eve's style was unique and often involved anime characters. Half Taiwanese, her mother was Asian, and her father was a lily-white with black hair Primrose. The anime thing was because she loved that stuff. Most days, she looked like an anime character herself.

"He had a radical office," Eve said. "In a building that would rent for bundles. He seemed on the up and up." Eve drove Austin a little too fast out of the parking garage and I had to bite my tongue to keep from shouting something about Mario Andretti. You'd think that surviving a car accident would make me feel I'd cheated death and was invincible. It didn't.

"The first thing I want to do when we get home is investigate the deed. Tomorrow, I want to go look at the place." I doubted the house was much, although I did wonder if it was willed to me because it was haunted. That would be something.

"You want to drive to the Oregon coast tomorrow?" Eve sounded like she might have other plans. That was fine. I'd have Carlos take me to the house and describe what he saw. He knew words like dilapidated, rundown, eyesore. He even knew how to say holiday trailer if it was one. I had no idea what this house would look like but could imagine. It was free.

"Go do something fun tomorrow, Eve. Carlos knows how to find Oregon." It was only a four-hour drive.

"Are you joking? I want to see the place. I don't want Carlos using up all the ranky adjectives."

I snort-laughed.

Carlos was my tech expert, the guy who knew the most about recording ghostly noises at high frequencies, filming and mixing our weekly show to look like it wasn't engineered in a floating houseboat, which it was. He was essential for my business and a godsend, as much as Eve was with her abilities. Eve had two talents I needed, especially these days: her inherited psychic gift and her marketing abilities which, strangely enough, counted for as much in my business.

In our wacky Primrose family, we all had something akin to clairvoyance which made for predictable drama at family gatherings where everyone was reading everyone else's thoughts. Two years earlier, Eve and I had split off from the crowd of thirty or so after a particularly bad Thanksgiving and haven't been in touch with our overly-sensitive family much lately, except for Christmas well-wishing and the occasional comment on Facebook. This is how Eve and I preferred to view our family—from a safe distance.

Even after Harry's death, my mother told me that she'd "seen the accident." I almost punched her right then and there. Days later, I was tempted to ask why she hadn't told me, but it wouldn't bring Harry back. That, and Eve pointed out that my mother's abilities were spotty for no known reason and she was probably lying about the premonition. She'd predicted

Uncle Ogden would travel far this year and when he broke his back, we knew that this man wasn't going anywhere. My mother's clairvoyance could not be trusted, something the Primroses knew and that made Rachel about as happy as a caged wolverine. She'd been hungry for a good prediction and might have said she saw the accident just to get a score on the board. That was my mother.

With me on Eve's trusty arm, we walked to the top of the dock that led to my home, a 1500-square-foot houseboat that was Harry's pride and joy. He'd bought the place with money from his grandfather and we'd called it Floatville. We both loved living on the water with a view of the Seattle Space Needle on one side and a snowy mountain range in the other direction. Our views were very Pacific Northwest.

"Anything on the dock I should be aware of today?" I asked Eve.

"Clear ahead except for a floating cottage with fairytale window boxes." Eve had graduated from U of Washington in Communications and luckily knew how to expertly describe everything in sight. Her use of adjectives lately had skyrocketed to admirable levels, and I wondered if she kept a dictionary under her pillow at night. When I was a teenager, Eve seemed a lot younger. She'd follow me around at family gatherings agreeing with everything I said. Although there were five years between us, we seemed to have caught up in age these days.

With my recently purchased white cane which was a long thin stick that folded like a tent pole when not in use, and training from an Orientation and Mobility specialist, I headed towards Floatville tapping my cane in time to, "Bad Moon Rising," my mother's ringtone.

"Don't go 'round tonight, it's bound to take your life, there's a bathroom on the right."

"Maybe slow down," Eve cautioned. "And it's 'Bad moon on the rise.'"

I ended up at my front door and felt for the ghostly wreath that still hung there from last Halloween. The lights were hot, still plugged in, which I found touching.

"That was your best one yet!" Eve said with such enthusiasm I almost cried.

People were afraid I'd fall off the dock and forget I was a great swimmer, so I was determined to prove everyone wrong by navigating the dock like a pro.

"Gracias, my darlin'," I called.

Eve's optimism in the last months had kept me going, made me want to grasp something worth living for. If Eve thought I could do it, I supposed I could.

At least I wanted to.

I opened the door and entered my floating home as the new owner of two residences. Even if one was a shack riddled with rats, the idea was heady for a moment.

I owned two homes.

CHAPTER 2

The houseboat smelled like my patchouli air freshener. I was so much more aware of smells now that my eyesight was gone. And I did love the smell of patchouli.

My cane clicked on the hardwood floor as I set out for the desk near the window. Right foot forward, cane tap on the left. Left foot forward, cane tap on the right. Sometimes, I tapped out songs I was singing in my head. It made tapping more fun. It was just a silly game I'd taken to playing while I got used to the cane. A few days ago, I'd gotten so involved in tapping the song "Happy," I'd completely run into a shelf in the drug store. Eve was a screamer and that moment was no exception. I'd been taught to listen for the tapping echoes, but it was so much more fun to sing.

"Pie arr-alar la bamba," I sang. It was then and there I decided to name my cane. Yes, I would call the thing TapTap. It seemed appropriate and brought this long, thin helper into my family with a name. I found my way to the chair and plunked down, folding TapTap up into a short, stubby bundle.

No longer could I see the picturesque canal, the other houseboats and the colorful marina with a field of masts to the right. I knew the view well and remembered what my home overlooked. I had memories, something people born blind did not have, as my mother kept reminding me.

"I'm going to my room," Eve said.

I smiled in the direction of her voice. "Try to find a nice boyfriend," I said, in a Bronx accent. This was our running joke. Eve was on a break these days from relationships, which worked out beautifully for me, having her available when I most needed her. Eve's last boyfriend was a controlling loser who took advantage of her and had made an intervention necessary to convince her to dump him. Working for me, a needy blind lady, was a step up, something that made me feel pretty good on days when I asked Eve to find me a pair of clean underwear.

While waiting for my laptop to boot up, I realized I hadn't eaten breakfast. My last meal had been KFC the night before. Eve wasn't much of a cook and until I figured out how to slice food blindly, I was not attempting meals. I missed cooking. I did keep candy bars hidden in the bottom desk drawer, however, and found what felt like an Almond Joy with two lumps.

Next, I called my mother to see if she still thought Mrs. Giovanni died at the hands of her daughter. Just because I detested my mother didn't mean I didn't phone her to see what she was thinking at any given moment.

"I'm sure her no-good daughter poisoned her, or worse," Rachel said. "Mrs. G told me that they were fighting, and it got pretty bad. I have a feeling, but I'd like you to come by, see if Mrs. G wants to say something from the other side."

My mother had no idea I was broken. I hadn't told anyone that my abilities had left me like a cheating husband's wife. No one except Eve and Carlos. "Maybe tomorrow." Appeasing my mother today wasn't on my to-do list. If the police suspected homicide, they'd investigate. Also, I had good reason to ignore my mother's plea for paranormal assistance at Mrs. G's house.

My whole life Rachel had used me like sending a canary into a coal mine to test the air quality. The ability she didn't have and wanted was mine, something I often thought of as a curse when she'd take my barely adolescent self to haunted houses and leave me in the dead of night to find out what the ghost wanted. This is basically how she financed our life. We never had much but we usually had a roof over our heads, even if the roof sometimes belonged to one of the Primrose Clan. Then she discovered rich older men and our quality of life improved greatly.

Becoming a hired paranormal investigator in the last eight years was so much more credible than what my mother had me doing in place of attending high school. During one of our many knock-down, drag-out verbal battles in my adolescence, she'd once said, "At least I'm not making you turn tricks." I remembered storming from the room that day, knowing my mother would never be normal and because of that, I had a slim chance of turning out well.

She'd always been beautiful, like a movie star from the fifties, with her dark hair and bright blue eyes. But, in direct opposition to her lovely visage, Rachel swore like a sailor and married men for their money then divorced them faster than you could say, "Too bad there was no pre-nup."

I set to work on my laptop, feeling determined to do something that counted, besides inheriting a house that someone else worked hard to build, or buy, and maybe maintain. Just because I'd been raised a moocher, I wasn't without a sense of contributing. I was probably more aware of pulling my own weight because of all the favors I'd been granted in my twenty-eight years.

With screen reader software, a lovely female voice told me I'd reached my site online. After typing in my search, I listened to the woman inform me that the deed to the house on Smuggler's Cove was recorded at the Clatsop County Office. And according to the voice, the house was now owned by Bryndle Clementine Moody. Me.

How the hell did Belinda McMahon get my middle name? I never told anyone that abomination. I owned the house before I'd even signed the deed. Was that legal?

An email notification pinged on my laptop. It was from the lawyer. My first thought was that he'd written to say there'd been a mistake and the house was supposed to go to someone else named Bryndle Clementine Moody. But, no. The soft voice I thought of as Moneypenny read me the email.

I was instructed to send you this email one hour after you left our offices. It's from my client, Mrs. Belinda McMahon.

Dear Mrs. Moody:

I am trusting to you my most valuable legacy, knowing that your life has been based in paranormal experiences that many pass off as fabricated stories. I believe in your talent.

Cove House is blissfully haunted, and I want to leave this grand old lady to someone who will appreciate its many qualities.

It is with great joy I pass along my home to you. There's only one other request beyond keeping it for five years, and that is that you do an investigation. What you will find in Cove House might surprise you.

I'm counting on your expertise and generosity to help the ghost.

> *Sincerely,*
> *Belinda McMahon*

There was a catch! I knew it. But an extremely good one, it seemed. I'd inherited my own ghost. Today felt like Christmas, with me getting the best toy ever imagined. My heart pounded in my chest and I felt like punching the air in enthusiasm. What did *blissfully haunted* mean? I wasn't sure what to make of the letter, but the prospect of a ghost investigation where no one was hanging over my shoulder waiting for a report was appealing to me. In my business there's always a client, and demands, and a time frame, and sometimes disappointment.

Even though the house was mine, Belinda McMahon felt marginally like a client, but because she was dead, time wasn't a factor. Nor would there be disappointment at not finding a ghost. Occasionally, a client expected more ghost action besides me just sensing occupation and telling the ghost to move on. Some clients wanted to see the ghost themselves and I had to explain to them it didn't work that way unless they were psychic. Only a select few got to see ghosts. Not even Carlos and Eve were lucky enough to get in on the action, most times. Eve was on the verge of tapping into her inherited talent and I was trying to speed that process along. Carlos had the standard five senses. These days, I was down to five myself, possibly four, if my clairvoyance didn't kick in soon.

I texted Eve, who was twenty steps away in her bedroom, to tell her our exciting news about inheriting a house that was haunted and was now a hundred times more interesting. A thousand times.

Even if it was a two hundred square foot trailer, I owned a ghost.

Eve emerged from the other part of Floatville, the area with two bedrooms and a bathroom. "I knew it!" She sounded as excited as I felt. "Now we have two haunts," Eve said.

We'd recently been given the go-ahead on a restaurant investigation east of Seattle. The owner had emailed me about setting up the date to explore his haunted restaurant and I was excited at the prospect of gently working my way back to the land of the unliving. My calling card in the paranormal industry, if you can call a bunch of mediums and psychics an industry, is that I hold the honor of being the only ghost hunter who has ever captured a clear image of a moving ghost on video. A stroke of timely luck. The footage of a white apparition crossing a room in a Seattle warehouse went viral last year. It's five seconds of ground-breaking video. Non-believers said the tape was fake, that it had been doctored, but believers knew it hadn't. I was used to skepticism.

"Which place shall we investigate first?" Eve asked.

I hadn't felt anything telepathic since the accident and hoped it was because I'd been blocked by grief. For five months we'd been referring cases to another ghost hunter in Washington State, but now I felt ready to get an investigation on our books and uploaded. "Maybe The Eatery in Roslyn," I said to Eve. Our new case was a small restaurant less than two hours from Seattle in a town called Roslyn where a famous TV show was filmed in the 90's because the town resembles Alaska. The restaurant had a resident ghost—a female spirit that had been seen several times. I'd taken the case knowing it was a slam dunk for a skittish rider getting back on the horse and was hopeful we'd be able to help The Eatery's owner, Jim.

Although visiting haunted houses wasn't financially lucrative, our show on YouTube was and we needed to get product online after so much time of nothingness. Having a ton of subscribers on YouTube allowed me to pay two employees a decent wage only because I had sponsors and clicks and everything you need to get money on YouTube.

When I'd decided to take The Eatery case, I was sure the haunted restaurant would produce something wonderful and had been cautiously hopeful. But, having inherited a haunted house in the opposite direction, I was torn between two haunts now. Although Mrs. McMahon's letter was ambiguous, I was thinking that exploring my inherited house could be my psychic litmus test with no client watching me. It was an opportunity for me to see if what Carlos called my "loco mojo" was still alive. "First on the list, we'll check out the Oregon house with no formal investigation, then head off to The Eatery, see what that ghost has to say," I said.

It was with a glimmer of hope that I emailed Carlos to tell him my news of the inheritance and invite him to road trip to Oregon's wild coast tomorrow. I would figuratively look at my inherited property and if I felt the presence of a ghost, I'd be farther ahead than I was today. If I didn't feel anything, I'd deal with that at the time. Even if my inner sight had gone AWOL, Eve could handle things in Roslyn. Her abilities, although undeveloped, were strong enough in a situation where the ghost had appeared multiple times. She and I would play that one by ear having already discussed working in tandem to make it look like it was business as usual for Moody. Nothing wrong here, folks.

Carlos would film me lying my face off about feeling a ghost.

CHAPTER 3

On the drive to the Oregon coast, Carlos and Eve talked non-stop for the first hour. This was something I was used to, their compatibility, their shared experiences and friends. My two team members had dated briefly in college before they discovered they drove each other crazy when they were around each other long-term, as a couple. Their breakup had been amicable after only two months and a year ago when I'd asked Eve to find me someone with knowledge of how to use all the gear that was needed to measure paranormal activity, she'd suggested Carlos. He was a techie and what my family called "a believer" so when I'd told him the role he'd play in the grand scheme of Moody Investigations, he was all in.

"Very cool stuff," he'd said examining the equipment with a wide grin. "I love filming." Supplementing his income from an audio-visual part-time job at a high school, he was available to me nights between midnight and dawn and had jumped at the opportunity to investigate ghosts. "Muy creepy," he'd said in his half-English, half-Spanish way. Carlos was Mexican and into that Day of the Dead philosophy, so Eve and I knew he wouldn't mock us or wonder if he needed to call the men in white coats when we started channeling spirits.

Before leaving Floatville that morning, Eve had found what she believed to be my new house on Google Earth. I overheard Eve telling Carlos that the lot was isolated from the town and beach and every other tourist establishment that makes up the wild and wonderful Oregon Coast. "The property is ocean front," she'd said excitedly. "And if this is the place, it's not exactly a double-wide trailer, Bryn."

I didn't ask what she meant. We'd be there soon enough. Eve might have meant it was worse than a double-wide. I didn't know.

On the drive through Washington towards Oregon, Carlos and Eve kept a running narrative going of what they saw out the window, something I found touching. And helpful. I encouraged them to do this, all day, every day. Like I'd also encouraged them to wear cologne to keep track of their whereabouts. It all helped me picture what I was missing. If I smelled a light floral scent Eve said was called "Happy," and heard the footsteps of a ninety-five-pound person, it was Eve. When the footsteps were heavier, and I smelled Eau Sauvage, I was sure Carlos was close. He wore Nike running shoes which were harder to hear than Eve's army boots, but in my sightless condition I was learning to identify people by using other senses.

Every so often, Eve and Carlos got into spirited discussions that left them cursing and getting so frothed up, they had to be separated. Like now. Except we were in a van, a van I called The Marshmallow, and headed down a freeway to the next state. They couldn't go to their rooms for a time out. And Carlos couldn't slam a door in a Latino temper and not come back until tomorrow.

"I didn't say that you are a slob," Eve said. "Only that you don't do dishes until the health department comes pounding on your door."

"What do you think about buying a monitor that registers heat levels?" I tried to change the subject. Paranormal investigators, especially those with no telepathy themselves, monitor levels of everything from heat to electro-magnetic energy. Carlos even had a teddy bear he'd found on the internet that emitted white noise and made it easier for spirits to talk on that frequency and be heard. That was called Electronic Voice Phenomena, when a ghostly voice came through over the TV, radio or a walkie talkie. The short form, EVP, was easier to say. Sometimes with EVP, you had to guess what was being said behind the static but many times I'd heard ghosts speak their names or issue a warning like "stay away."

It was always a nice mix of validation and incredible fun when EVP came through. In the past, any equipment we used in our investigation was only backup, on hand to supplement what I determined with my ghost-magnet personality and telepathy. Recently though, I'd wondered if the tech stuff might take center stage in importance.

"It couldn't hurt to measure heat levels more effectively than us just saying, 'it's really cold over here.'" While Carlos explained how ghosts sapped heat and electricity from around them, I tried to engage, but my mind was elsewhere. I was lost in thought, having now distracted my road trip companions. Today, I was worried that I might enter a known haunted house and feel nothing. And that Eve would feel everything. I didn't begrudge my young cousin her gift. I just didn't want hers to be our only gift.

"And there, mis amigas, is the Pacific Ocean," Carlos announced.

We turned south and were now traveling along the coast and although I couldn't appreciate the view, the smell of the ocean was strong. I had my window cracked and the scent might as well have been expensive men's cologne complete with a photo of a handsome movie star on the poster. I loved the ocean with a passion. Always had. Harry and I had taken our scuba certification on our Hawaiian honeymoon. The instructor said I was a natural and I believed she didn't say that to every customer from Seattle, just because that was her hometown too. I felt comfortable near the ocean and in the ocean and wondered as I breathed deeply if my house would smell this good or if it would smell like the rats that probably lived there. Although I could also smell rain in the air, we hadn't seen a drop since we'd left Seattle. (I had to stop saying stuff like that. *They* hadn't seen a drop. I hadn't heard there'd been any drops.)

As we closed the distance to Cove House, my companions narrated the view and I was able to imagine the little white roadside diner with the red trim, the neon sign flashing "Beachy Stuff," the vintage Ford truck we passed driving thirty in a fifty-five zone, and the field of grass dotted with white long-legged birds. The salty smell made my heart rate quicken. For good and bad reasons. We were getting closer to the house. The anticipation of psychic judgement day had me in limbo. Either I'd be devastated today or elated, depending on whether my clairvoyance kicked in. The words "five senses" kept popping into my head as we closed the distance to the house. Five senses rolled around in my head like a wish, a chant, a mantra. I wanted at least five.

After almost an hour on the coast, we slowed and came to several stop lights in the town of Smuggler's Cove, which sounded charming. The GPS on Eve's phone directed us out of town to the house. Carlos slowed The Marshmallow and we turned.

"You have reached your destination," the phone voice said.

"This must be the driveway," Eve said in a whisper.

"Trees on either side, dense forest, the road looks like crushed seashells, one lane." Carlos sounded preoccupied.

The wheels crunched on the driveway.

"I see a clearing . . . and the house is dead ahead," Carlos said.

"Are you serious?" Eve said on her way to a yelp. "Oh, my gods, will you look at . . ." her words trailed off.

I waited, depending on my companions for so much.

"The house is enormous. It looks like a hotel built in the last century." Eve's voice was loud and high.

"The century before that," Carlos corrected, ever the history major.

"There's a sign reading, 'Cove House.'" Eve added.

As the van slowed, I rolled down the window and took a deep breath of sea air. I could hear the ocean crashing on rocks in the distance. "Is it on a beach or a cliff?"

Eve answered. "Probably a cliff. The house and trees block the view from here."

The van came to a stop and Carlos whistled. Eve opened the sliding door from the back seat. "The place *looks* like it's haunted. It's grey with white trim, three floors with a widow's walk."

"Probably six thousand square feet," Carlos added. His mother was a real estate agent.

We'd gotten very little information from the lawyer yesterday but the address, the key, and later, the letter from Belinda McMahon. In all fairness, the lawyer knew nothing because he had not been Mrs. McMahon's lawyer in her last years of life, only someone she hired to do the transfer of title and notification that I'd inherited a house. Seldom Wrinkled was innocent.

Eve described the structure in front of us as she slipped from the van. "It's mega-humungous. Floatville would fit into it five or six times. Ominous looking. In need of TLC."

"Belinda McMahon lived here by herself?" Carlos asked.

"No idea," I said. We really knew nothing about the woman. Except that she had a bad heart.

Eve touched the sleeve of my jean jacket. "I'm no HGTV expert on architecture, but this joint looks Gothic. It's got eight steps leading to the front door near a gazebo thing with a pointy roof."

I tried to picture it.

"It almost looks like two tall houses of three stories with a center tall house leading up from the front door. Like three sections. The roof looks mossy but no holes. Not that I can see."

"Nope, not from this angle," Carlos agreed.

"There's a balcony off a room on the right side second story. The house is trimmed with lots of detail, almost like a dark doll house but it looks like it needs repairs. The third floor has another balcony with a pointy railing, again on the right side. There's a crow sitting on the roof staring at us." Eve's voice wandered off.

I thought of the crow sitting on my shoulder the day before. "Do you feel anything?" Usually, at this point I had a niggling feeling of paranormal activity. Today, I did not.

"No," Eve said. "I'm busy trying to describe this place."

"You're doing a great job," I said. "Let's go see the house." The ground under my Frye boots felt soft, grassy. Things like this were becoming second nature to me. Determining what I hadn't seen by what I could hear, touch and smell. Taste had advantages but not right now, unless you counted a slightly salty taste on my lips.

As I took Eve's arm, Carlos moved in to offer his arm on my other side. Apparently, the staircase was wide, and we could walk three abreast. We walked towards the house on an even sidewalk. "No garage, I assume."

"No," Carlos answered. "But there is some sort of building off in the trees to the left. Maybe it was a place to leave the horses. This place would have been built before the automobile, I'd say."

"What kind of trees?" I could smell the tangy telltale scent of evergreens.

"Mostly coniferous. I need to study flora and fauna," Eve said. "I'm going to guess pine trees but I'm drawing a blank because I suck at tree identification."

"Douglas Fir," Carlos said. "They have big, chunky bark and there's Hemlock with droopy tops."

I imagined Eve looking at Carlos like he might be lying but I couldn't be sure. There were exactly eight stairs and I made a note that they were tall stairs, not the usual height for steps. At the top, we walked five steps to the front door and I disengaged from my companions, the key now in my hand. I felt the door, determining it was made of wood with a glass window at the top. The doorknob felt like it was made of brass, oblong. I inserted the key, turning it to the left to where it clicked. My right hand turned the doorknob and the door to my future opened.

I took a deep breath pushing the door inwards.

My companions were silent, but I could hear Carlos breathing. He was a heavy breather, I'd discovered lately with my heightened hearing. My hands shook as I stepped into what I believed to be a hall. The house smelled musty, old, neglected. This wasn't from any psychic determination, just something I surmised through smell. I reached for a wall to the right and felt wainscoting at waist level, probably wallpaper above the wooden paneling below. "Describe what you see, Eve."

"We're in a six-foot-long hall that opens to a circular area with a . . ." she shrieked. "A chandelier that looks like it's going to come down any minute."

"Is it hanging by an electrical cord?" I didn't want us walking underneath it.

Carlos interrupted. "It looks fine. Why do you do that Eve? Make her all scared when things look fine?"

"I hate those things."

This was how their arguments started. I intended to defuse it. "Don't start." My boss voice sounded appropriately firm. "If it's not dangling, then continue with your description, Eve."

"Beyond the circular foyer are stairs, one, two, three, four, five, six, seven, eight, nine of them to a landing half-way up to the second floor where two different staircases go to the right and left to the next floor. It's all wooden, red rugs, dark, dank. On our left is a paneled wall with two doors. The first one is closed, the second one seems to be half-way back and it's open. On the right is a double door to what looks like the living room. I can see furniture covered in sheets."

"Let's go in there first." I hadn't felt anything yet, something that was very unusual for me in a haunted house. I tried to be hopeful. As we walked forward, I heard Carlos go on ahead, his sneakers barely making a sound on the carpeted floor.

I flicked TapTap open and started the song "Margaritaville", making half circles from side to side on the floor in front of me. Proper cane technique dictated you listen, not sing. I wasn't there yet.

"Waiting away again in Margaritaville," I sang.

"Is the carpet wet? It smells musty in here." I stopped and reached down to feel the carpet runner. It was dry.

"I'm not feeling anything. You?" Eve whispered.

"Nothing." We crossed the threshold to a room that felt big, Margaritaville still playing in my head, my cane tapping. "Working for that log shaker of salt," I sang. I closed my eyes, just past the doorway and put out my arms to draw in anything that was passing by, something I'd done for over a decade.

Nothing.

I tried not to panic.

"Let me know the second you feel anything, Eve," I said.

"So far, zilcho."

Carlos moved around the room. I could hear the click of his electromagnetic reader. The clicks were slow and even, meaning it hadn't spiked. At least my lack of clairvoyance was in good company. My Braille watch told me it was just after five p.m. and these days, that meant we had another hour until darkness. Ghosts like the dark.

Although we hadn't planned to stay overnight, now that we were here, I was thinking of changing the plan. Today's agenda included only looking at the house, taking stock of what I'd inherited, and driving back. We'd talked about another trip to Oregon after our Roslyn investigation, especially if the house looked habitable. And apparently it was highly habitable, more than a condemned bungalow with no furniture and rats running the place.

"Is all the furniture covered in sheets?"

"In this room, yes." Eve moved from my side. "There is a big curvy window out to the front. I can see where The Marshmallow is parked. It's started to rain harder."

I'd already heard the rain tapping on the windows. Once during an investigation, we'd gotten a clear tap-tap-tap on a window nearby, the ghost desperately trying to communicate, but this tapping today was too regular and sounded just like rain. Since I'd gone blind, I was amazed at how I'd relied heavily on sight, not giving my hearing a chance to show off what it could do.

Eve continued. "The furniture looks old-timey. Uncomfortable. And there's a piano by the window. One of the 3-D ones with the top propped up."

I smiled at her description. "A grand piano."

Carlos' voice came from the other direction. "Lots of windows, big heavy drapes and a fireplace."

I heard someone play a few bars of "Margaritaville".

"Slightly out of tune," Carlos said. I hadn't known he played, but his talent didn't surprise me. Carlos was an enigma.

"The mantel is dark wood, wide, with two sets of silver candelabra," Eve said quickly, probably not wanting Carlos to take her job describing everything. "There are paintings around the room, mostly of scenery. Maybe oil paintings."

"The lights don't work," Carlos said.

I'd heard him clicking. "I'll have the power turned on tomorrow. If we're going to do a thorough investigation, we'll need it."

"The carpet is red in here, too; the furniture striped, red, black and gold."

"The ceiling is high."

"No chandelier thingy."

"Table lamps."

"Five hundred square feet."

"A door back here."

"A half-burned log in the fireplace."

"The door leads to an office."

"A couch."

"Low table in front."

I was wishing Carlos and Eve were always this competitive about describing our surroundings. "Well done, you two, let's go across the hall." I found my own way to the door, not having moved much, a trick I was learning in the months since I'd lost my sight.

We crossed the foyer, making a wide arc to avoid walking under the chandelier. I tapped out "The Lion Sleeps Tonight," singing softly. Eve was on my arm and I'm a terrible singer, I've been told. Soft was better.

Eve opened the door to a room that she described as a library. "Like the narrator's office in the *Rocky Horror Show*," she said. This room had a rolling ladder to retrieve books from the higher shelves. Again, dark wood paneling, scenic oil paintings and a fireplace. Two armchairs flanked the fireplace, "for reading," Eve said. I lowered myself to sit in one, feeling the cold leather and upholstery pins at the armrests.

Still nothing came through to suggest the house had a ghost.

I stood, felt my way to the book shelves, and sneezed from the dust.

We continued.

29

On the first floor was a grand dining room with a table that had seating for twelve people, a kitchen with modern appliances that looked "out of place," Carlos said, and a large pantry with canned foods that had expired a year ago. More than once I wished I could see this house but didn't voice my frustration to the two people who were my eyes. And more than once I thought that Harry would have been fascinated with the place, having graduated from Seattle University with a minor in history. He'd have been tickled to see the ornate woodwork that Eve described as looking like "The board game Clue."

When I climbed the stairs with Eve's arm on one side and a banister on the other, I turned left at the landing to mount the second staircase. "Is it decrepit or pretty?"

"Pretty," Carlos said, already at the top. "Did you ever see the movie, *War of the Roses*?" Like that."

"*Downton Abbey*." Eve was hell-bent to outdo Carlos.

"Not that big, Eve."

"The look, not the size, Carlos." Eve sounded annoyed. "The house is dark because the light is fading and we're away from the windows, but this was a grand place. I don't feel spirits, but I bet balls were held here, or at least those big parties where everyone arrived in horse-drawn carriages."

At the top of the stairs, I realized that if my companions didn't like me, it would be easy to push me down the stairs or murder me and I wouldn't see the crime coming. I was so vulnerable these days, relying on two people who were on my payroll. I made a mental note to inform them they weren't in my will.

"At the top, there's a landing and windows that overlook the front of the house, open to the stairs, red carpet with a design. There's a huge table in the center of the landing and vase, no flowers. Also, stairs going up to a third floor."

We approached the table where I walked around its perimeter, feeling my way. I then found the window, felt the size of it and the ornate woodwork around its edge. "Can I follow this wall?" I asked, my right hand on the wall beside the window. Essentially, I was asking Eve if I continued walking with my hand on the wall, would I bump into anything before I came to an end.

"All clear," she said.

I arrived at another wall sooner than I thought and turned.

"This is a hall leading to the back of the house. There is one on the other side of the stairs, too. Rooms are off the hall on both sides once you get past the stairs. Stay on the right side and you won't fall down the stairs."

I walked the length of the hall, my hand on the wall to feel the doorways. There were four rooms apparently. The house was deeper than I'd imagined. I didn't turn left when I reached the end but came back. From the other side of the house I heard the even clicks of Carlos' monitor. He hadn't found anything yet.

Returning to the front of the house, I kept my left hand on the wall. All doors were closed.

Eve opened the door closest to the front and I stopped. "What do you see?"

"It's a large room running half the length of the house. Windows on two sides. Judging by the furnishings, I'd say it's a dude's bedroom. The colors are dark green and gold, there's a canopied bed, a dresser, writing desk, fireplace and at the far end is like a family room with couches that do not look comfortable, with another fireplace. There is a small chandelier, yikes, heavy velvet drapes, tied at the five-foot height, dust on everything but not so thick to indicate someone hasn't been in here in years, maybe months." Her footsteps clicked on hardwood as she went deeper into the room. "Oh!"

"What?"

"Carlos! Come here!"

I walked two steps into the room. "What is it?"

Her pause told me what I hadn't wanted to know. And what I had wanted to know. She felt something.

Carlos ran through the doorway, the monitor beginning to click quickly as he entered.

"Tell me, Eve." My words sounded defeated.

"Someone died in here. It was a woman. She's close, maybe watching us. Her death was sudden. A murder."

Eve would have her eyes closed, trying to pull everything in.

I reached out to try to do the same, my emotion so strong that I was sure my desperation would block any spirits that lingered. The gift eluded me. I was without sight. Both kinds.

"What was that?!" Eve jumped, her footsteps scurrying towards me.

I waited.

"I felt a tap on my shoulder," Eve whispered.

Carlos would be recording this, filming for the show, and I hoped he wasn't capturing footage of the blind woman standing uselessly at the doorway waiting for her young cousin to supply her with information.

"Are you here with us?" I said. "We mean you no harm. We know this is your house." It always helped to give the ghost the house. Let it know that you are the intruder. "We felt you. Can you give us another sign?" My assistants knew enough to never speak during this part of the investigation. I was the one who did all the talking to the spirits. So far, that was how it was done, anyway. Things might have to change.

We listened. Being patient was part of being a ghost investigator. Carlos moved around the room, his meter slowing to one click every few seconds. He'd be wearing headphones to record anything captured on his high-power microphone. He might even have had the teddy bear strapped to his utility vest, I didn't know. It always looked comedic to see this Mexican dude carrying a teddy bear in amongst the high-tech tools.

"Can you communicate with us? Tell us you're still here?" When the meter clicked frantically on investigations, I was never the one to feel useless. I was a conduit for ghosts and always had been. But just now, Eve had pulled in the ghost of a woman who'd been murdered. That would be reason for a spirit to need help crossing over. Murder precludes ghosts from leaving this world entirely, sometimes keeping them between here and there, not able to be in either world. I'd often thought it must be a lonely life.

Ten minutes later, after prolonged silence, I called it. "Nothing more?"

"Correct." Eve was now standing by Carlos, probably staring at the meters and monitors.

"What did you get Carlos?"

"An eight," he answered.

Eight was good. Definite ghost activity. The number matched the clicks we heard. "Any vocals?"

"Nothing I heard."

"And Eve? Describe what you felt." I crossed my arms without thinking, realizing this was the opposite stance I used to pull in ghosts. I guessed I was done trying, subconsciously, at least.

"Only what I said. I felt a presence when I entered the room. It was colder than downstairs. I got the impression a woman died in this room. I felt a faint brush on my shoulder." Her voice sounded disappointed but not nearly as disappointed as I was at that moment, having felt absolutely nothing. Not even the hair on the back of my neck stood on end.

"When did you feel things return to normal?"

"When the clicking stopped," she said.

"Okay, resume normalcy."

This was my command, like telling soldiers "at ease." While Carlos and Eve compared notes excitedly, I measured the room with my right hand on the wall, walking to the corners, past the window, around a table and back to the door. "Wallpaper or paint?"

"Wallpaper," Eve said. "It's kind of dark in here so I can't see clearly but the wall against the hall looks like a painting, a mural of a house on a cliff and a stormy sea. The house might be this one." Her voice wandered away, presumably walking along the wall. "Carlos, have you got a flashlight?"

I heard Carlos approach her and then Eve screamed.

"Eve?" I instinctively put out my arms.

"She's fine," Carlos said. "What do you see Eve? I can't see it."

"There's blood on the wall, like someone was killed right here. Where the sea meets a stony beach under a cliff. There's a house on the cliff that looks exactly like this one. And the blood is at heart level, making a smear to the floor like someone was killed against this wall and her body slid down the wall."

I walked over, daring the furniture to get in my way. I put my hands on the wall and Eve moved them along another two feet.

"Right here." Her breaths were coming fast. "It's still dripping."

I tried to empty my mind of everything--the accident, Harry, my blindness, sadness—but nothing stirred in me. In the past, I'd sometimes relied on drinking whiskey, which had worked well to loosen me up. For a medium, this was a shameful admission, but it was something I'd discovered years ago, while drunk at a party and ghosts were bombarding me with their problems.

Pulling a flask from my jacket pocket, I twisted off the cap and took a long swig of Crown Royal. It burned going down and I made a face. I hated the taste but, in a pinch, it worked the best. "I'm going to ask you two to leave the room for five minutes."

Footsteps shuffled out and I heard the door close softly.

I steadied myself. "If you are trying to contact us, please know we want to help you. Belinda McMahon gave this house to me and asked me to help you." I waited, my eyes closed, even though it made no difference at all. I put my hands on the wall again, palms flat against the mural I couldn't see. "Did you die here? Who killed you?"

I heard Eve and Carlos whispering outside the room. My acute hearing could even pull in that, something I would have traded for eyesight. Even terrible eyesight.

"Please come to me. Tell me that you're here. I want to help you." I stood very still waiting for a tap on my shoulder, a voice in my ear, a rustle of the drapes, anything, but as I stood in what had been described to me as manly quarters, nothing came to me.

This life would be so different without my gift.

CHAPTER 4

Gathered around my kitchen table in Floatville, discussing our plan for the week, I told Eve and Carlos I'd promised my mother I'd come by later to see if I got anything sinister from Mrs. G's house. I expected nothing to present itself to me, given my state of nothingness, but knowing my mother, there'd be no rest until I did as she asked.

Mrs. G's house was empty, and Rachel had a key, so I imagined she wanted me to walk around inside and try to contact her dead neighbor. I'd give it a go, but being empty of medium juice, I anticipated the only feeling I'd get was the creepy feeling of walking around inside a dead person's house at night without permission. I told my mother I'd come over that night.

"That's more like it," she'd said, which had me grinding my teeth.

Maybe I'd walk in with no hope of feeling anything at Mrs. G's and get something awesome because I wasn't trying.

"I'll take you over," Eve said, setting down her cup of coffee.

I couldn't deny that I was excited about investigating again. Not pulling in ghostly thoughts sucked but at least there'd been activity at Cove House, just like we hoped. Potential loomed for Eve, at least. I could take it as slowly as I liked, use the house to keep trying.

"Tomorrow is Roslyn?" Carlos asked.

"Aye aye. All hands on deck," I answered in boat talk. Our preliminary investigation at The Eatery gave me hope because the ghost had appeared many times to people without psychic abilities. Even patrons of the restaurant had seen that ghost.

Eve had made Huevos Rancheros with the tortillas and salsa Carlos' grandmother had sent over and we ate while talking about our upcoming cases. Wraps, I'd discovered, worked better than chasing food around a plate with a fork. These days, I put almost everything in a wrap to eat it. I even wrapped a baked potato recently, complete with sour cream, bacon bits, chives, and butter.

"When's Hodor coming home?" Carlos asked.

"Twenty-five days," I said.

Every day without Harry's dog was a difficult one. I'd always wanted a dog, ever since I could remember and when I met Harry and heard he had a Black Lab, the package deal seemed too good to be true. These days, Hodor was training to be a service dog, something everyone who was near me in the last five months recommended. I'd sent him off with a lovely lady from Seattle who'd taken him to a school in Oregon for training at a place called The Seeing Eye Service Dog Academy. Truthfully though, I didn't care if he learned anything there, I just wanted my dog to come home. Hodor was a connection to Harry.

I'd researched the history of Cove House that morning and discovered enough about the original inhabitants to believe that there had been some shady business dealings coming from the owner. Smuggler's Cove had a museum in town and I'd spoken with the curator, a woman named Joan Hightower who seemed agreeable to divulge what she knew.

The builder of the house, a Mr. Cuthbertson, had made his money in timber, and with a wife who hadn't exactly wanted to come west, he'd built her the home of her dreams. Then, she'd died of typhoid fever. A child, too. The house was sold to a shipping man named Stevens when Cuthbertson moved back to Philadelphia.

I hadn't mentioned a ghost to Mrs. Hightower, only that I inherited the house from Mrs. McMahon and would be in the area next week to visit. "I'm trying to find out all I can about the history of the house," I'd said.

"Cove House has quite a story," Joan said, her voice reaching an excited level. "I'll look forward to meeting you. I think you'll find Smuggler's Cove a charming little town."

I didn't mention that I'd already been to look at the house, nor did I mention that Eve described the outside of the museum as a dumpy little log cabin.

"Do you plan to move to Cove House?" Joan had asked.

"I'm not sure," I'd said, trying to be evasive. I didn't know who knew what about me or Belinda McMahon in the town of Smuggler's Cove.

I told Eve and Carlos about my conversation with Mrs. Hightower while we ate breakfast. "She might be useful to us," I said, hopefully.

"We have five thousand new subscribers since Oregon," Carlos said, his mouth full of food.

We'd loaded some teaser footage from Oregon to indicate a new case was being filmed. "That's pretty good, right?" I asked.

Eve was in charge of this area, and of our social media accounts. She also kept track of our marketing. "We just loaded the footage, and our numbers will climb for the next few days," she said. "Five thou is nothing to sneeze about."

As the talent, I never wanted to talk money, numbers, or advertising. Or do the camera work. I just wanted to show up, contact ghosts, and clear the house of spirits. We all had our areas of expertise. Originally, Harry had helped me set up the channel, and as it grew, I found I needed to hire someone who knew more than I did about YouTube. Eve was that person. Then, when Carlos came on board, our video of the ghost went viral and the business took off.

"The new footage we uploaded," Carlos said, "looks spooky."

"Like I said, Carlos, don't post any shots of me, even from the back, unless I look like I'm contributing something. I don't want our fans to know I'm blind or to think I've lost my loco mojo." Something dribbled down my chin and I wiped it with a napkin from my lap.

"I'm extra careful," Carlos said. "The latest footage was the outside of Cove House, a walk to the bedroom, and Eve talking about the bloody wall. Less than five minutes, and only your voice and the back of you on camera. We're building suspense."

"That should satisfy them for another few days," I said.

A noisy motor boat drove by my dock too fast and we felt the house bob on the waves. The speed limit off the dock was five knots and that sucker was doing at least twenty. Harry used to report anyone speeding by the house if he was home to catch them. I could only shake my fist in the window and hope they saw me.

"Tomorrow, we'll have more footage from The Eatery and can load shortly after, maybe space it out, in case we get nothing at Cove House." Carlos was speaking with his mouth full, something that drove Eve to distraction. I imagined the look of disgust she was giving him across the square wooden table.

The main room of the houseboat served as a sitting room and small dining area, connected to the galley across a counter. Being the chef of the family, when I'd moved in with Harry, I'd reworked the kitchen, putting in a pretty backsplash, painting the cabinets white and outfitting the space with pots and pans and gadgets I'd collected over ten years of cooking. I fully intended to get back in that little kitchen to cook elaborate meals again.

I took my empty plate to the kitchen, listening to Eve and Carlos talk about the ghost in The Eatery and wondered if I even needed to go on this one.

For now, I'd continue to go along, manage things. Moody Investigations was my business and I had to show up, even if it put extra work on my two employees leading me around.

***

Mrs. Giovanni's house was dark, completely shut up, with no one inside since her death. Her daughter lived twenty miles away in another town, and as my suspicious mother and I let ourselves in the back door and moved through the kitchen, I felt guilty for intruding this way.

"Sorry Mrs. G," I said.

"What are you sorry about?" my mother asked as we entered the living room. "She'd want me to be sure she died naturally."

My mother had brought a flashlight to light her way to the bedroom and I took her arm for guidance. It was a small rambler, like my mother's house, but this place smelled musty. Like no one had lived here in years. Not clairvoyance, just an observation.

"Her bedroom is in here." We turned left and my mother all but shoved me through the doorway. "Are you getting anything?"

I took a deep breath and concentrated on the bed in the room, presumably in front of me. "Mrs. Giovanni, it's Rachel and Bryndle. Are you here with us?"

"Terri? Did your no-good daughter poison you?" My mother had a nice way with words.

I didn't feel anything but wanted to give it more of a chance. I took two steps forward until my thigh hit something. I reached down to feel the edge of the bed. I rested my hands on the top cover. "Mrs. Giovanni, are you here? Rachel thinks you might have been poisoned. If that's true, can you give us a sign?"

We waited.

Nothing.

Finally, my mother, who had the patience of a puppy, added her two cents. "I'm feeling that she was murdered." My mother did not have the ability to pick up on stuff like this. That's why she'd always sent me in. I knew she was lying but decided to leave it at that.

"I'm not getting anything. Let's go." I turned, and Rachel took my arm to guide me out of the room.

"I got the feeling her daughter killed her for the insurance money," Rachel said as we left the house.

"OK, then tell the police you suspect her daughter."

"Didn't you feel that, Bryndle? Maybe you weren't trying."

We walked back towards my mother's stylish rambler with the timber and river rock front. "I tried but I'm a bit rusty, I guess." I wasn't about to tell my mother that I suspected my ability had flown out the window with my eyesight. "I haven't done anything in months."

Eve was waiting on the porch for me. "Find anything?" she asked.

Rachel took this one. "I got the sense she was murdered but Bryndle didn't try."

"I tried. Come on, Eve." I wasn't about to hang around and get into it with my mother. "And you're welcome. I drove all the way over here to help you."

"For nothing," she said.

"I can't help it if I'm out of practice." My voice sounded like I was ten-years-old.

"I'm just saying your livelihood will be in the toilet soon enough if you don't pull up your big girl pants and get back into it."

Eve took my arm. "See you later, Aunt Rachel."

We turned and walked to the car.

"Tough love, Evelyn," my mother called to us. "Gotta be tough!"

"Is she saying," I whispered, "that she's trying to dole out tough love or that you should?"

"Or that she's tough to love," Eve giggled as we got in Austin and drove away from my toxic mother.

CHAPTER 5

It was just after one a.m. and the three of us were standing in the darkness of The Eatery, an historical building on the main street of the tiny town just over the mountains from Seattle.

Eve had described the outside as "an old red brick building, old windows, two-story, with a big sign advertising the 'Best Food in Town.'" Jim the owner, was with us, "looking nervous," Eve had just whispered in my ear.

We walked past a long bar on the left and tables along a wall on the right, and turned to descend steps into a second room with a large stage at one end. I was wishing I'd worn sensible shoes but with the camera rolling, I needed to look like Moody, who had a very distinctive brand that straddled Rock Chic with Punk Witch.

Tonight, I'd worn a clingy long dress of purple jersey with a high collared trench coat and tall boots to look the part of someone with so much talent it was ridiculous. It was my belief that just as many followers tuned in to see what I wore as those to see if I found a ghost. Comments on our show's site often remarked on my weird clothes, strange hair, or gaudy jewelry. I wasn't just a medium and ghost whisperer. I was an entertainer fashionista who took my role as such very seriously. I wanted to give the people a show.

The restaurant smelled of dinners served hours earlier, not the usual dank, mustiness of a haunted building. The restaurant was not warm, the heat having been turned down for the night, but it was not the chill of a paranormal presence.

The second room we walked into was full of tables and booths. This was where the ghost usually showed up, on stage, or over near the stairs leading to the basement. The apparition of a young woman in a long dress had been seen many times in the last decade but most recently two months ago. The ghost had frightened a pair of women heading to the restrooms in the basement. They'd seen the apparition floating up the stairs towards them, then turn and make a hasty retreat through the wall.

Frightened customers were never good for business and although Jim didn't necessarily want to get rid of the ghost, he wanted something, he said. "Maybe just to know more about her. I can't decide if she's good for business or bad," he'd said when we arrived.

Carlos set his equipment on a table at the back of the stage room while I sat on the edge of the stage, listening, waiting, kind of trying. Putting mental feelers out to see if anything was drifting by, like a sea anemone in a current, hoping to pull something in to feast on. So far, I was still hungry.

Eve had told me the room was dark and everyone but me wore night vision headsets. Jim wore mine. I'd decided to be seen on camera without the goggles and that would explain if I bumped into something. Carlos was on the other side of the room clicking, plugging in, clearing his throat, breathing in his rumbly fashion.

When Carlos gave the signal, we moved to the hall near the staircase. I got a fix on where the camera was located and stared in that direction. Carlos adjusted so it looked like I could see that camera and when he said the shot looked good, I nodded.

"Remember, don't get the Frankenscar in the shot."

"The makeup is taking care of that," Eve said. "It's hardly noticeable."

"Then, count me in."

"4, 3, 2 . . ."

"Investigation number sixty-five, The Eatery, Roslyn, Washington, March 23, 2018." I paused so Carlos could edit that part out of the uploaded film. "Good Evening, Mood Peeps. We are in the town of Roslyn, Washington at a restaurant called The Eatery. The ghost appears to be a woman who floats around after hours and was most recently seen on the stairs to the basement during working hours by two customers on their way to the restroom. The spirit appeared as a white, transparent apparition in a long dress who disappeared through the wall when encountered. Jim, the owner of The Eatery, has asked us to investigate. It's just after one a.m. and we're ready to begin. Carlos, set your meters. Mood Peeps, prepare to get freaked out."

This is how I began every video. And, this was the argument Eve used to encourage me to attend tonight's session, saying I was the star of the show and they needed me as part of the team. Earlier, her tears of disappointment made me take her in a hug and vow to do my best to contribute tonight in Roslyn.

Carlos walked the room, taking readings while Eve stationed herself over by the door leading to the basement. I presumed Jim had obeyed my order and was seated at the back of the restaurant. We didn't usually let the clients attend investigations, but he'd seen the ghost several times in six months and she seemed to want to tell him something. Maybe Jim would draw her in.

Twenty minutes in, I did another spot from the stage.

"Count me in," I said in the darkness.

"4, 3, 2…"

"I'm going to try to contact the ghost." I paused and looked off to the right. "Is anyone out there who'd like to talk to us?" I said. "We've traveled here to help you, to meet you. Are you here?"

We waited.

"My name is Moody. I talk to ghosts to figure out what they need. Who are you?" I listened. Several times, we'd had a ghost say their name at this point and captured it on EVP. Some ghosts loved to distinguish themselves.

"Are you with us tonight? Let us know if you can hear us." I held my breath, listening. "We mean you no harm but only want to know who you are."

Ghosts often made objects rustle, or drop, or tap, but as we listened, we heard nothing.

"Do you know Jim, the owner of this establishment? Jim is here tonight to make contact." I raised my voice. "Jim, say something."

He spoke from the back of the room. "Ah, hello. I want to know who you are and what you're doing here. Are you listening?" His voice was shaky and didn't hide his embarrassment at talking to a ghost. Speaking to someone not of this world did feel strange at first.

Eve's footsteps moved away from me as she headed down the hall towards the stairs to the basement.

It wasn't unusual to take a long time to make contact, or to not get anything at these investigations. Sometimes, it took days and sometimes the ghost just did not want to communicate. Not every investigation produced a ghost. But in the past, all my investigations had produced information about the ghost, back when I had strange feelings as soon as I opened the door.

So far, I felt nothing from the other side.

Carlos and Eve continued walking around the restaurant. I didn't move much except along the length of the stage. I could hear Eve head down the stairs and was impressed with her bravery. When she first started to work with me on investigations, she often stayed behind me for protection. A year later, she was walking down creepy old stairs trying to find the ghost of a two-hundred-year-old building. My heart swelled with pride.

Carlos moved from one side of the room to the other, the clicking of his EMF meter my gauge of where he was. He was too far away for me to smell Eau Sauvage.

I called towards the hallway. "Eve, try speaking to her."

Although Carlos had the toys-- the meters, and recorders for electromagnetic levels, and disturbances in the atmosphere that might signal something close, Eve and I were mediums and relied on talent. Or had. Now, I was wondering if I should carry equipment. My talent was on an extended lunch break. Maybe I'd end up carrying around one of those Boo Bears, tied to my utility vest while Eve dressed in flowing clothes and leather.

I heard Eve's timid voice on the stairs saying something like what I'd just voiced to the room about making contact. Her footsteps were light, getting softer as she disappeared down to the next floor.

"Are you with us?" her soft voice asked.

Carlos headed towards her. I monitored all this from my stationary spot in front of the stage like a general sending soldiers out to battle.

"I feel you with me." Eve said, her voice louder than usual. "Are you here?"

I moved along the stage, my hands feeling the speakers, a table and finally the wall. I'd left TapTap in The Marshmallow, not wanting it to sneak into a shot, but was wishing I had it now just to get around the corner and into the hall. I bumped in to a table and chairs, then continued, trying to follow Eve's voice.

"I hear you," Eve said. "Is that your name? Carrie?"

Eve must've gotten something on her microphone. I heard nothing as I inched around the door to the hallway.

"Carrie? Or Mary? Are you with me?"

We waited. Carlos was now closer to Eve, his monitor clicking frantically.

It was like fishing, in some regards, all this waiting, hoping, then a tug and off you go.

"We mean you no harm. Are you troubled or stuck here?" Eve's voice was high, her words fast. "Ouch! Don't do that." Her steps shuffled up the stairs. "Someone pinched me."

I couldn't get to the stairs fast enough to help but put my hand out for the wall and moved along. "Carlos?"

"I'm on it," he said. "Evie, let me see."

Seconds passed while I waited for words to hear she was fine.

"She pinched my arm," Eve said. "Carrie, I know you're here with us. Can you tell me if that's your name?"

Silence.

Finally, Carlos spoke. "You have a big mark where she got you."

"No pinching, Carrie," I said. "You'll have to find a way to contact us without hurting us or we leave."

Our policy was that if a ghost was violent, we called it, gathered our information, and made a new plan. If it was a minor attack, we went back in based on what we knew. "Back up here, please," I said to Carlos and Eve. Once I'd even been inhabited by a ghost in an old Victorian house. That was freaky-ass cool, and only cool because the bad entity eventually left me, and we exorcised her from the house. When she was inside me though, I'd felt her sorrow and frustration of being murdered and buried in the wall of a house under construction.

I heard Jim clear his throat, now close to me at the entrance to the hall.

"Jim, has she ever hurt anyone before?"

"Not that I know of. Well, there was that time my girlfriend had bruises she couldn't explain after working the bar."

A pinch wasn't bad but if this Carrie was intent on hurting, we had to be careful. That was a whole different investigation when ghosts got through to perform physical damage.

While talking in the hall, the door to the basement suddenly slammed shut. Carlos' meter was going off frantically and Jim yelled.

"I see her."

I stood near Jim but felt nothing. Until the ghost passed through me, leaving me feeling frozen and desolate. "She just went through me," I said.

Then Jim felt something cold on his neck. "She touched my neck! It was frozen like . . ."

"Has she ever touched you before?" I asked him.

"Never. It felt like a popsicle on my neck. Very cold."

"Can you still see her?"

"No," Jim said, his voice reflecting the fact he was either shaking from fright or shivering from the popsicle touch.

Carlos' meter was slowing, telling me that the ghost had left. "She's gone," he said.

"Carrie, are you still here," Eve asked.

We listened and I heard a jingle from the next room. "Where's Jim?" I asked.

Eve told me that Jim now stood by the door, looking ready to go. I'd heard his keys jingle.

One last ditch effort had me asking for more. "Breaking through like that is much better than pinching," I said. "Thank you for messaging us."

Ten minutes later, we called it.

As we headed towards the restaurant's front door, my hand on Eve's shoulder in front of me, I had a strong sense that told me to turn around. It was the first time I'd felt anything remotely like this in months. I wasn't going to ignore it.

"Just a sec," I said. Carlos and Jim were up ahead talking. I turned and cocked my head, wondering what this was about or if I'd dreamed up this request to look back. My eyes were open wide, even though I had no reason to expect I'd see anything. But I did.

The room was dark, almost wavy like it was underwater, but I could make out the configuration of the tables, the bar on my left, the depth of the room, pictures on the walls, and the doorway to the restaurant part we'd just come from. In less than a second, I saw all this.

And something more. My vision settled, and I saw clearly in the dim light as the figure of a person disappeared around the doorway to the restaurant.

"Hello?" I said.

Eve was behind me, ushering the men outside.

"Do you want me to see you?" I whispered. I continued to stare at the doorway into the stage room, my sight leaving me. Soon, all I saw was the blackness I was becoming accustomed to. The apparition was gone and with it, my ability to see. But I had seen the bar, even the photo of a car on the wall to my right.

"Eve?" I turned and headed towards the door, now knowing that nothing stood in my way if I stayed on the carpet runner.

"Did something happen?" she asked.

"I'm not sure," I said, not wanting to share my news yet. Not trusting that it happened.

"Did you see a young woman wearing a long white dress?" she said.

That was the thing. What I saw was not a woman in white. My ghost was a man. A man with long hair and if I wasn't mistaken, he wore a suit jacket with tails.

My ghost looked more like a pirate.

CHAPTER 6

This was a huge game changer. I'd seen something. Yes, it was fuzzy and dark, but I saw the ghost of a man disappear around the corner and presumably down those few stairs from the bar into the restaurant.

I fricking saw something!

As someone trying to come to terms with the black hole in front of my face, this was monumental. I didn't tell the others. Instead, as soon as we stepped outside, I made a decision. I asked for a few moments alone in the building. Everyone but me left the building and as they stood talking on the sidewalk, I went back into the restaurant and clicked the door closed, shutting out my companions. I was ready to play hard ball. I needed this ghost. The man I saw wasn't Harry who had a slight build and blonde hair.

I walked a few steps forward, now knowing what my terrain looked like.

"I saw you just now. Come forward, you coward, and present yourself." Challenging words like this might appeal to the ghost's sense of manliness, honor, and swagger. I didn't know. I was winging it. "Don't hide like a coward!" I said forcefully. "I saw you." I stood my ground, holding my breath, hoping with everything I had that somehow, I'd get through to the other side. That the spirit could hear me, and it wasn't just my imagination fooling me into thinking I'd seen not only the layout of the bar and restaurant, but I'd seen a man ducking through the doorway, his coattails swinging as he hastily retreated.

I carefully walked towards where I knew the doorway to the stage room was, felt for the edge and descended the four stairs into the restaurant. "I know you're in here. Show yourself." The vision in front of me was total blackness, a scene I'd come to know well. Still, I kept my eyes wide, looking around the room for anything to show me that I hadn't imagined what I'd just seen through my eyes.

Taking two steps forward, I bumped into something and my hand went out to feel the back of a chair. I clutched it with both hands. "Please, whoever you are, I need to see you again." Should I throw everything out there, just in case?

"My husband and I were in an accident that took his life. And took my sight. I seem to have lost my former ability to speak to ghosts, to draw in spirits." The room was deathly quiet. "But, I just saw you. Or, I think I did. Now, I'm not sure." I was rambling, but if the ghost was listening, I figured it didn't hurt to lay everything out on the table. "I saw you, a man in a long dark coat, and you wore boots. You have dark hair. You moved quickly as if you didn't want to be seen, but I need to see you." Hot tears burned my eyes. "I want to know there's hope. Please show yourself."

I wiped the tears from my cheeks and waited.

Soon, I heard the restaurant's door open quietly in the next room. Footsteps I knew to be Eve's crossed to the top of the stairs.

"Bryn? Where are you?"

"I thought I heard something and came in here," I lied. I would keep my secret for now. "We can go."

Quietly, she approached and took my elbow to help me up the stairs. We walked silently through the bar and out the door to the night's cold air.

"I wanted to give it another small effort. Without equipment." I'd done this before and my fellow investigators knew that this worked sometimes.

"Ready now?" Carlos asked softly.

"I am. Jim," I said, addressing our client, "we'll get back to you in the next few days after we've had a chance to analyze all the data."

"Jim left five minutes ago," Eve said. "He said to tell you thank you."

I might have been embarrassed talking to someone who wasn't present, but I was learning to get over these moments. With my crew, at least. "Let's head home then," I said and waited for Eve to give me her arm to lead me back to The Marshmallow.

"I'd like to do a second investigation here in the next week or two. Pinching is troublesome." I slipped into the passenger seat, clicked my seat belt closed and heard Carlos enter the back of the van where he'd be busy on the drive home, checking our footage and playing back the findings on his meters. He had a desk area back there, like some FBI surveillance agent.

Thinking about what I'd seen in the bar made my heart feel lighter, like I'd just had very good news.

Being able to see the bar, the pictures on the walls, the groups of tables and chairs, the liquor bottles behind the bar, it was heady, as if I'd had a glimpse into the future and things were looking better. Did I get my vision? If I got my psychic sight back, I might be able to communicate somehow with Harry. It was a long shot but would be something to keep me going at night when I mourned the death of my best friend and lover. I so wanted a sign from my Harry.

I spoke from the passenger seat with more vigor than I'd had recently. "Good job everyone. Is it sore where she pinched?"

"Carlos, shine a light over here. I want to see if she left a mark," Eve said from the drivers' seat beside me, holding out her arm. "Yes, it's sore."

A few seconds passed. I waited and then, "Whoa! That's a good one," Carlos said.

"What is it?" Someday their descriptions would come without me asking.

"I have a bruise," Eve said, "the size of a silver dollar, not much, but verification that I was pinched."

In the joy of having seen something through my eyes just now, I'd forgotten that the ghost made a very nasty crossover from being passive to harming Eve. It was never good when they communicated this way and both my crew knew this. "What were you saying just before she pinched?" I asked.

"We might have to play it back," Eve said.

"I remember." Carlos had a photographic memory, something that was very handy. "You asked her if she was Mary or Carrie.

"Maybe she hates being called by the wrong name," I said. "It was vindictive, whatever the case."

"Whoa!" Carlos said. "Listen to this Bryn!" He put the headphones on me and I heard a static voice speak. "My love," it sounded like.

"That's just before Jim yells and runs away," Carlos said.

"What is it?" Eve asked, now driving.

"I'm pretty sure Jim's ghost said "be careful, my love" just before she touched his neck. Is that what it sounded like to you, Carlos?"

"Si, that was what I thought, too."

"Do you think the ghost is in love with Jim?" Eve asked. "That's so romantic to think that a ghost is in love with an Alive. Unrequited love and forbidden love all in one bundle."

"Have you ever heard of that, Bryn? Where a ghost falls for an Alive?" Carlos' voice was close.

"I have. It's not unheard of when a ghost is rattling around a house and becomes enamored with its captor, so to speak." I wasn't sure if that was what we had, but Jim's girlfriend had bruises.

"If that's the case," Carlos added, "Jim is going to have to break up carefully with this ghost if she's a pincher who can slam doors." He laughed but I didn't. We might have a jealous ghost on our hands and that was never easy. Or fun.

We turned onto highway I-90 and sped back to Seattle, the van going up to seventy miles per hour, a cruising speed that scared me for good reason. My facial scar twinged. The cut on my face was something I was trying very hard to ignore. My lack of sight helped me not to see it but periodically, Frankenscar hurt.

"I wonder why she told Jim to be careful." We'd completely ignored that part of the ghost's message.

"If she loves him, maybe she fears he'll marry his girlfriend or something," Carlos offered from the back of the van.

Eve touched my left shoulder. "I know you felt something back there, Bryn. What was it?"

Did I need to keep this from them? Probably not, but I wasn't ready to release my news to the world just yet. "I had a thought, more than a feeling, that if I was alone in the room, I might appeal to the ghost, seeing she pinched you and obviously had some animosity towards you." That much was true.

"What did you say?"

It was selfish, but I didn't want to train Eve to do what I did. If she knew all my tricks to summon spirits, it diminished my worth and even though I was not worth much right now as a paranormal investigator, I was worth more than I was an hour ago.

"I said that I understood her pinching you. Sometimes you're a pain in the ass."

Luckily, they laughed at my feeble attempt at a joke.

***

Two days later, on the way to the Oregon coast, I realized that if my mother found out Eve's ability to contact spirits was up and running, she would summon her to Mrs. G's house sometime soon. "By the way, Eve," I said. "Rachel will be on you like a hungry tiger when she finds out you have felt spirits, so keep that secret under your hat. Don't tell her anything unless you want to be used and abused," I cautioned.

"Too late," Eve said from the backseat of The Marshmallow. "She called last night, and we got talking. She asked if you'd picked up on anything at Mrs. G's and I misheard her and told her I hadn't felt anything. I'd need to be inside the house."

I groaned. "Is that where you went last night?" Eve had gone out and I assumed she had a social life. Or at least girlfriends to hang out with like any normal twenty-four year old.

"Bryn, I think Mrs. Giovanni was murdered."

Carlos whistled from the driver's seat in admiration.

"What makes you say that?" I didn't want to block a murder investigation, I just didn't want to work with my mother on one.

"We went in the bedroom and I felt it." Eve sounded almost frightened to tell me.

"What did you feel?"

"I sensed that Mrs. Giovanni was forced to do something."

"Her daughter?"

"No, someone else. A dude. I don't know."

"Did you tell my mother this?" Rachel was dating a cop and I was sure she'd be foaming at the mouth about this to her new boyfriend.

"I did. I haven't spoken to Aunt Rachel since last night. I'm sorry I went all undercover." Eve's voice was small inside the big noisy van.

"You should have told me, Eve. Just because I didn't get anything doesn't mean she wasn't murdered. I'm glad you helped. What did my mother say she was going to do with this new information?" I was curious.

"No idea, but she looked like a werewolf during a full moon when I left."

I was tempted to call my mother but didn't want anything to ruin our day of discovery at Cove House. "I'll call her tomorrow. I'm sure she's pleading her case with the boyfriend cop right now."

Of course, it was raining when we pulled up to Cove House. March on the Oregon coast wasn't known for sunshine. It wasn't drizzling either but teeming sideways like the world was coming to an end. The wind off the ocean was driving the rain to hit the van door noisily. That's how I knew it was raining sideways because it wasn't until I asked what the weather looked like that Eve supplied the bad news we would get drenched when we walked from the van to the front door.

"Carlos, get the bumbershoot," I said. "I'm not sure the clothes dryer in the house works yet." We'd brought clothes and food, enough for a few days, but still, I wanted to keep as dry as possible on the walk in. After all, I couldn't run up the stairs to avoid the downpour. I still had to take my steps carefully.

"According to the house specs there's a laundry room with washer and dryer off the back veranda," Eve said. "But who knows if it's hooked up."

I didn't know. But I had a feeling we'd all know soon enough. We hadn't yet spent a night at Cove House, having decided last time we were here that we needed to bring clean sheets for the beds. Once we'd finished with the bloody bedroom investigation, our little group had headed back to Floatville for the night.

"I'm parking The Marshmallow as close to the house as I can without driving on the grass." Carlos said.

"There is a rectangle of lawn, about thirty feet deep with a sidewalk leading from this driveway's ending," Eve said.

"I've got a perfectly functioning hood on my coat," I said. "You guys take the umbrella."

"Carlos has the megabrella and we can all fit underneath," Eve said. "Let's take those wooden stairs slowly. They might be slick."

Harry had given me deck shoes once as a joke because Floatville never left the dock. We weren't sure how seaworthy our house was even though it had a motor at the back if we ever needed to move it. This morning, I'd considered wearing them, but I'd gone with my Frye boots and a raincoat with a hood. I reached back to pull the thing over my spiked hair. Although lately I'd traded in my signature teal blue spiked hairdo for something more easily controlled, today I was full of hope and had transformed to Moody by styling my hair in signature spikes by applying gel to the top and pulling the ends to make them stand up. My hair was part of my brand and Carlos would undoubtedly pull out the camera and start filming today. I didn't want to look like Bryndle, the normal person, if that happened. Before we'd left Floatville, I'd asked Eve if I did a good job, before the gel dried.

"Perfecto," Eve had said.

I didn't know if she was lying to make me feel better but assumed she wouldn't let me go on camera looking non-Moody. Strange and crazy was OK, but not plain and boring.

Today, might be a big day for me and I wanted to be ready. Even if I didn't have another miraculous incident, as I'd come to think of getting sight at The Eatery and seeing a ghost, I was going to try as hard as I could here, say the same words, stand the same way, and try to summon a damned ghost until we left in six days.

I slipped out of the passenger seat and with Carlos on one arm and Eve on the other, we made our way up the stairs, laughing about the torrents of rain coming down.

Inside, we shut the door on the afternoon weather and I slipped off my coat. "Is there anywhere to . . .?"

"Right here on the right," Eve said, breathless. "It is a four-hook thingie." She guided my hand to hang up my coat.

I felt the wall and the thingie. "Good to know," I said, thankful for Eve for the millionth time that day.

Then Eve screamed.

I listened for a clue to what happened but finally had to ask. "What is it?"

"The chandelier," Eve said.

"I'll be damned," Carlos added. "You were right, Eve. That sucker is coming down."

"It's hanging by a wire," Eve said. "Five feet from the ceiling now." Eve's words were whispered.

If that thing fell, not only would it break what I imagined to be a beautiful piece and damage the floor, but someone could get hurt. "Carlos, call someone, an electrician, I guess. See if they can come right now. In the meantime, try to figure out how to either cushion its fall or secure the thing. And don't anyone walk under it."

Carlos was probably on his phone looking for electricians before I finished my sentence.

"Let's get a cup of tea and sit in front of a fire, Eve." My jeans were damp from the walk up the stairs. "Maybe stick a mattress under the chandelier," I called as Eve and I walked to the room on the left, the library.

I ran my hands over the wood pile, fumbling and feeling as Eve watched from a chair by the fireplace. I'd told her I would make the fire and she could light the match. I imagined her biting the inside of her lip as I worked. Being a good fire builder had been my joy on family camping trips even though my cousins would shout out their spot-on predictions as to how many matches my fire would take. It usually only took one if you prepared the fire correctly.

I crumpled some newspaper and made a teepee over the pile of paper with sticks, adding larger ones to make a bigger teepee over the smaller one. I'd toppled the thing once and had to rebuild by feeling around for the sticks. I was learning the hard way to be a lighter touch. And patient. Eve was probably learning to keep her trap shut, to not tell me where everything was located, like playing that game you're getting hotter, colder, you're freezing, you're red hot!

"I'll start the tea," Eve finally said, leaving the room, probably taking the matches with her.

I worked on the placement of the sticks and kindling then settled back into the chair, waiting for the sighted person to come back and light the match.

My phone rang Creedence Clearwater's "Bad Moon Rising." Although I knew better, I took the call.

"The police are looking into the murder of Terry Giovanni," my mother said. "So that ball got rolling, thanks to Eve."

I took a deep breath.

"I still need to move in with you for two weeks." She said the last part like it was no big deal.

"I inherited a house," I said, mostly to throw her off.

"Yes, I sensed that." This was one of my mother's favorite lines and was often not true.

"Bull," I said. "Where is it then?"

My mother took a moment, then answered. "I happen to love the Oregon coast." She said this like a victory lap was in order. "Why didn't you tell me you were moving, Bryndle?"

"I'm not moving. I now own a vacation house."

"Why didn't you tell me you inherited a house?"

I intended to ask Eve if she'd told Rachel about Cove House. And if so, how much she'd divulged under the duress of her evil aunt. Eve was often caught between me and my mother and I never blamed her for caving in and revealing everything she knew, not once Rachel got going. "Maybe I didn't tell you because I'm still very upset with you," I said. "Ever since you told me you'd foreseen the car accident." I'd decided to use that zinger for the next few years when my mother acted hurt.

"You know we can't interfere with premonitions." My mother spoke like I was being ridiculous, not defending my right to know an accident would take my husband's life.

I didn't actually think Rachel had experienced a premonition where she'd seen my husband and I in a car accident in which a Hummer came around a corner without stopping, slammed into our Smart Car and almost crushed the driver's side. Rachel often lied with bragging at the center of the lie but her insensitive proclamation of foreseeing the accident justified my ignoring her for months.

"I'd like the address for your Oregon house. I have to leave here for two weeks while they exterminate."

"When?"

"On the eighth."

It was the twenty-fifth. "Stay at Mary's, why don't you?" Aunt Mary lived on the same street only five houses away but would never allow her sister to bunk with her for even one night, let alone two weeks. And not because Mary was in a wheelchair from an explosion at the State Fair that she blamed my mother for. It was because growing up with Rachel had been a special kind of hell for her younger sisters, and Mary only took Rachel in very small doses.

"Mary's busy. You have two residences and Eve says the house in Oregon is large. I'll come there. It'll be fun."

I couldn't imagine a world where a visit from my mother would be fun. I was sure my mother had already decided that the next Primrose family reunion would take place at Cove House, especially if Eve had let slip that the place was large with a big yard.

"Did Eve tell you she helped me last night?"

My mother sounded braggy and I felt gaggy. "She did."

"She was very helpful, that girl."

I imagined my mother wondering how she could capitalize on Eve's talent now that she'd discovered her niece was fast-tracking her extra sensory perception skills.

"The police are looking into it. I had to tell Ron that it was you who felt Mrs. Giovanni was murdered."

"What the hell?"

"You have street cred in the psychic world where Evelyn doesn't." My mother's words sounded unfazed by my tone.

"Mother!" This was typical for my mom to twist things to her advantage.

"I'm looking forward to seeing your house and spending time with you. We've been off lately, you and I, and we need to get our mother/daughter vibe back and secured. I'm going to help you clear your chakras."

I doubted my mother knew how to clear anything but a room with her thoughtless comments, so I needed to put an end to this visiting idea. "There's no guest room. Just rooms with bloody ghosts and rats. I

68

have to go," I said hearing Eve come through the swinging door from the kitchen.

"Call me later with the address," my mother said, obviously not concerned that I didn't want her to fix my chakras. Or the possibility of rats.

Eve set down the tray of tea and I told her my mother had been on the phone. "The police are supposedly looking into Mrs. Giovanni's death now that she's assured them a credible source has confirmed her neighbor died mysteriously. And, Rachel has invited herself here. To Cove House." I heard a slight intake of breath from Eve. "I can't imagine how my mother knew I had inherited a house in Oregon." I was a terrible actress but tried my best not to show Eve I knew she'd betrayed me to my nasty mother.

"Big regrets," Eve said, handing me a warm mug of tea. "I'd make a terrible spy. Me and singing canaries have a lot in common."

I took the mug, which was not scalding hot, but barely tepid. Eve was trying so hard to do good by me, and her sweet efforts softened the edgy mood left over from my mother's phone call.

"You know I have no defense against your mother," Eve said. "She corners me, and I turn to Jell-O."

I knew this about Eve and had once vowed never to leave my poor cousin in a room alone with my mother. Rachel is not for the faint of heart, or sweet-mannered people. I'd once come home from a free camp I sent myself to, only to find Rachel conducting her own kind of camp with my swimming teacher from the local Y. She'd convinced him to teach her to swim in my Aunt

Mary's above-ground pool even though he'd insisted he didn't teach adults. Poor guy hadn't wanted to teach someone who apparently did not own a bathing suit, nor did he want to get involved with her after the lesson concluded, but the young mom was just "too irresistible," he'd said to the Y a week later when they fired him.

"Rachel needs a place to stay in two weeks and I don't want her at Floatville. That place is too small, and her fangs and horns would get in our way." I imagined my mother with devil's horns and a smile crept across my lips. "I suppose we could deposit her here with the ghost and come back later," I joked. Rachel's talent was not ghosts. If we left her here for a week, I seriously doubted she'd even know there was a ghost.

"I'm surprised you'd let her stay here without you," Eve said.

"What do you think she might do?" I was curious.

"I don't know. Scare away the ghosts," she chuckled.

Eve lit a match and soon got my fire started. When the wood was crackling and popping I sat forward to warm my damp jeans. The house was understandably cold with the thermostat kept at sixty-five.

"You did a great job building the fire," Eve added. "Every day you get more independent. When your clairvoyance returns, you may not even need me, instead just sensing where everything is. Have you ever thought of that?"

I had. What was more likely? Gaining my clairvoyance or my sight? Even though it had been five months, I wondered if I still had a five percent chance or if it diminished every month my sight didn't return. Was I at one percent now? "It would be nice if I could function that way, sensing everything around me with no need for sight," I said, more for Eve than myself. "Then I might not even need my braille teacher." I wasn't fond of the woman who came to Floatville every week to teach me how to read braille.

Betty Sumar had admonished me for not practicing enough at her last visit and often spoke to me like I was a child. Consequently, I acted like a child around her and called her names when she left. Names like Stinky Sue, (I'd once detected faint body odor on her) or Betty Big Pants. After being treated like a sub-human it was rewarding to close the door on Mrs. Sumar and say, "I'll practice my fingers off this week, Mrs. Colonel Ugly Big Nose." I didn't actually have any idea if her nose was big, little, or broken sideways, but all these little games I played with myself gave back tiny smithereens of power to someone who was feeling diminished. I'd persisted with the braille lessons, not because I needed braille for much of anything in this day and age of technology, but because a blind person without knowledge of braille was considered illiterate and I was not going to have that label put on me without a fierce fight. Not after losing so many other things in the last months.

Eve slurped her tea quietly from the other chair by the fire. "Joan Hightower, the Smuggler's Cove Museum curator, called you just now and it was forwarded to the biz phone. She'll stop by tomorrow morning."

I nodded. I was anxious to hear all the details of Cove House and how the McMahons came to own this place. "Maybe she can shed some light on the bloody wall upstairs."

Just then, Carlos entered the room to say that an electrician couldn't come until tomorrow. "I dragged two mattresses downstairs to lay under the dangling chandelier, just in case."

"How much do you think the chandelier is worth?"

"I bet that thing is at least a ten thousand dollar antique." Carlos said, then went off to where he'd set up his equipment in the library.

Eve and I opened our laptops and set to work with her reading my emails and me dictating to her. It was so much easier than my turning on the screen-reading software and depending on Moneypenny reading line by line.

Luckily, I was proficient at tapping on the keyboard without sight, but I still had Eve proofread all my correspondence in case my hands got on the wrong line and it read like gibberish.

While we worked, an email came in from the lawyer, saying that another letter had arrived at his office today from Belinda McMahon, postmarked after her death. Who had sent that? The lawyer wrote that he'd either send it on or I could call his assistant for a read through.

We called right away, Cove House being the most important thing on my mind as I warmed myself at the drawing room fire.

Dear Mrs. Moody, I'm sure you're wondering why an old lady you've never met would leave you this house and I'm sorry I didn't explain more in the first letter. I had to be sure you would accept the house and if you're reading this letter, I guess you did.

As stipulated in my first letter, I do not want the house sold. If you choose to abandon Cove House, and I seriously doubt you will do that, given the treasure you will find inside, it will revert back to the lawyer who has further instructions on what to do with my Grand Old Girl.

As someone with exceptional abilities, I'm counting on you to uncover the mystery of Cove House and investigate the offerings to the fullest. I'm thinking it will take some time, but I'm confident that you are the perfect person to do so.

Good luck, my dear, and I hope you have the time of your life inside the walls of this fascinating house.

Belinda McMahon

PS: By the way, there are stray cats living in the coach house. They are feral and won't bother you.

I thought about what was said for two beats. "Send the letter on by snail mail," I said. "And please email me a copy."

We hung up with the lawyer's office and I heard Eve's fingers tapping on her laptop.

"I like cats. You do too, right Eve?"

"Yupper." She was still tapping. "But Carlos . . ."

We both knew Carlos was terrified of felines. Unnaturally terrified.

"I'd have to guess the mystery in the house has to do with the blood against the wall in the bedroom. I wonder why Belinda said it would take some time," I said.

"To hear Mrs. McMahon, it sounds like this house is Disneyland for mediums."

Easy for Eve to say. She had most of the clairvoyance now, which unfortunately was a fraction of what I used to have. But, I hoped it was enough to lead us to set things right with this house.

As I listened to Eve's fingers flying across her keyboard, I composed my questions for the museum curator tomorrow. I'd want to ask her not only about the house's history but if she knew why Belinda had singled out me specifically when there were lots of psychics in the Pacific Northwest who would be delighted to take on this project. Psychics who didn't have a following, a show, notoriety. And psychics who hadn't lost the ability to speak to and summon ghosts.

But then, Belinda McMahon would've had no idea before she died that I was a dud. I'd been the rock star of ghost hunters.

CHAPTER 7

It's a strange thing when you wake, open your eyes and see nothing—something I still was not used to. I woke feeling well-rested after going to bed early. The night before, we purposely did not try to summon any ghosts. I was exhausted, Eve had a headache, and Carlos was happily binge-watching a Netflix series.

I slipped out of bed and remembered I'd been dreaming of walking on a beach covered in seashells. Big conch shells and nautilus shells. At the far end of the beach a man in a sarong was blowing the conch, like he was summoning me to a luau. I ran towards him. In my dreams, I can see, which makes me look forward to going to sleep every night. In this dream, the colors were vibrant and clear, and when I woke to blackness, I had to remind myself not to be disappointed but instead be grateful for the dream.

I had a good idea of what my bedroom looked like, where everything was, thanks to an hour of walking the floor with my hands out and feeling everything my fingers could reach before bed. I'd chosen the bedroom at the top of the stairs on the second floor, across the foyer from the bloody bedroom. We'd joked that maybe we should invest in a baby gate for the top of the stairs. It had been me who said that. Eve and Carlos hadn't laughed. Someday, they might laugh at my self-deprecating humor about being blind, but not yet.

My room had a queen-sized bed and was furnished in a floral pattern, I'd been told. It wasn't as large as the bloody bedroom but had a fireplace, and a sitting area and was plenty big enough for me. The dresser drawers were empty, and Eve had reported that all rooms had been cleaned and cleared of personal items leaving no reminders that Belinda McMahon lived here recently. Unlike the room with the blood, this bedroom was not old-fashioned but more modern in design, which suited me fine.

According to Eve, my bedroom had a window overlooking the side yard and the coniferous forest beyond. The grounds at the side of the house were wild looking, no lawn, no upkeep needed, and in her description, Eve had used the words "scrubby bushes and rocky terrain."

I dressed in what I believed were my favorite faded jeans and a T-shirt that read, "Twirlin' On Them Haters," layering on a heavy sweater, and found my Frye boots I'd decided to wear in the house. This monstrosity of a house did not lend itself well to flip-flops, my usual footwear of choice inside. Although my room had a fireplace, I'd decided not to light it except in Eve's presence.

As I brushed my hair, the spikes now out from my before-bed shower, I considered growing it to shoulder length. I couldn't be sure my cowlick at the back of my head wasn't doing weird and wonderful things back there with the four-inch length I now had on top. My fingers couldn't feel a cowlick. Maintaining a funky hairstyle had gone to the bottom of my chore list, these days but luckily, Eve helped when I needed to look edgy for the camera.

I left my room, carefully found the banister and got myself to the first floor. My phone told me it was 7:43 am, too early for anyone else. Knowing that I'd be awake before the others, I'd had Eve set up the coffee maker timer last night to start dripping at 7:30. I could smell the coffee as I walked the hall, one hand on the wall, one hand tapping my stick in front of me to the tune of, "Locomotion."

"Everybody's doing a brandy dance now, Come-on Lady, do the Locomotion."

I remembered the table and chairs being in the center of the kitchen and the coffee maker on the counter off to the left behind the fridge which Eve had said was "stainless steel, state-of-the-art."

Seated at the table with a cup of coffee with what I assumed was the cream we bought, I wondered if talking out loud to the ghost might reach anyone. Especially at this hour of the morning. Ghosts like the night. The witching hours between midnight and three seem to work best if you are looking for a ghost. The fewer people, the better, and if the lights are on, you are less likely to find one. There are ghost rules, although it had been my experience in the last twenty years since I'd discovered that some of the things I see are not actual living people, that rules don't apply in every situation. However, for investigative purposes, we start after midnight, in the dark, with three people, sometimes splitting up to allow the ghost to break through in the quiet dark and be seen.

It's my belief that many ghosts are willing and enthusiastic to break our barriers, but it's difficult. Moving an object or shutting a door takes much effort on the part of the ghost and that's why spirits often disappear after a sighting. They put everything they have into making contact and then the connection is broken when they can't maintain it.

Nevertheless, I sat at the kitchen table in the daylight and spoke softly to the ghost in case she was listening. "My name is Bryn Moody. My husband died recently, and I want to reach him. He is Harry Moody. If you are listening and there is any way you can contact Harry, please tell him to give me a sign." The coffee mug was warm in my cold hands. "If you find Harry Moody, please tell him I love him, I miss him, but I'm going to be okay." I'd been whispering these words out loud for months except usually I addressed my speech to Harry directly. Without any response. Today, I tried talking to any old ghost who was listening.

I paused, trying to hear verification I'd been heard--footsteps or a tap on the window. There was nothing but the sound of the refrigerator switching on, something that had me nearly spilling my coffee in fright.

"Is anyone out there? Can you hear me? I want to make contact. I know it's very difficult to cross over but can you tap on something, or give me a sign you're with me?"

I waited but nothing happened. As a paranormal investigator, I was fully used to asking questions that never got answered. I'd spent years trying to get signs from ghosts with no response. But this was different. If

Harry was still with me, not yet crossed over, I wanted desperately for him to tap on the window or make my hair flutter in the stillness of that kitchen.

"I'm going to sit here and drink a cup of coffee and if you can, tell me that you're here." A thought came to mind. Maybe something was changing, something visual, but I couldn't see it. I decided to lay all cards on the table.

"I'm blind. I can't see anything since the accident that took my husband. And I used to be able to feel the presence of spirits on the other side but now I can't. I've lost two senses. But my hearing is very good."

I sipped my coffee, set it down and . . .either something brushed against my hair or . . .

I reached back to nothing, waited, listened.

Finally, I reached for the mug of coffee and my hand went through empty space. The mug wasn't where I'd left it. I carefully moved my flattened hand in front of me to find the mug, sure I hadn't set it anywhere but directly in front of me on the table.

Nothing.

I stretched further, deeper along the table and swept my outstretched arm slowly in an arc across the table top.

My mug had disappeared.

"Did you move my coffee?" I wasn't scared but highly excited that the ghost might have done this. It meant I was being listened to. I can't deny that I hoped it was Harry. My heart beat with the hope my funny husband was playing a trick on me. "I'm going to put my arms down now and you can return the mug. When I lift my arms up to the table again, I hope my coffee will be there."

This game would appeal to a ghost with a sense of humor. I hoped our ghost had such a thing. I did not hear the mug sliding across the table, but then, I hadn't heard the mug leave the table either. Had a heavy mug levitated? If so, that would be fricking amazing. I lifted my arms to the table and made the same sweeping motion from left to right. My mug hadn't returned.

Reaching out my arm, I swept farther, but found nothing. I sat silently for several minutes, wondering what I could possibly do to engage the ghost, if in fact he or she'd removed the mug from my grasp. "I wish I had that coffee cup. I really enjoy that first cup of coffee and don't want to get up to find another one."

I waited, took several deep breaths, cursed the fact I couldn't sense anything and battled the frustrated tears that threatened. A ghost was taunting me, and I hadn't even had my first cup of joe for the day.

"Thank you for telling me you're here." I pushed the chair from the table and found my way back to the coffee maker. Two mugs had been left beside the appliance and my hands found the second one. I repeated my earlier efforts of pouring myself a cup of coffee with cream.

Sitting down at the table, I first took a sip, then set the mug in front of me. As I pulled my hand away my right hand brushed against something. I carefully felt for whatever was on the table.

It was the other mug. Returned. With lukewarm coffee inside.

Either I was going crazy or I'd just made contact.

Maybe even with Harry.

***

Eve and I stood at what she described as a big-ass curvy window facing the ocean as she told me what she saw.

"The fog's gone and I can see the big pond. It's dark blue and stretches forever to the horizon."

"Eve, please tell me you know that's the Pacific Ocean."

"Affirmative," she said. "In front of this window, is lawn, if you can call it that. The grass looks like the gardener died way before Mrs. McMahon."

Sometimes her descriptions were so raw but so visual.

"There are huge rocks, boulders, near the edge of the cliff and I'm guessing it might be a long way down to the water. On the way far left is forest, on the right is scrubby bushes and trees. It's sandy."

"How far from the edge is the house?"

"I'm bad at this, you know that," Eve apologized. "I'd say the width of a soccer field, maybe."

That worked for me.

The doorbell rang, something we hadn't heard before. It was a melodic tinkling of notes and then we heard Carlos yell from the foyer, where he was working with an electrician to fix the chandelier.

"I'll get it."

There was a part of me that always worried any doorbell would bring my mother, but I had to think she was busy driving her boyfriend Ron crazy with Mrs. Giovanni's investigation and probably didn't want to leave town until the bug zappers kicked her out of her house. "Mrs. Hightower, probably," I said. The museum curator was expected any minute. "Shall we go see," I said, realizing too late that I'd said something that mocked my blindness. I wouldn't be seeing if it was Joan Hightower. I would be hearing or maybe smelling, if she wore perfume. I held out my hand and Eve took it to set on her arm. We walked towards the front of the house.

"Mrs. Hightower," Eve said as we approached the voice of Carlos welcoming someone to Cove House.

"Hello. It's lovely and also strange to be back in the house."

I recognized Mrs. Hightower's voice from the phone.

Eve turned us to walk a half circle around what I assumed was the no-go zone under the chandelier, while Carlos offered to take our guest's coat.

"Thank you for coming to visit with me," I said. "You probably can see that I'm blind. It's something I'm still getting used to having happened only months ago." I didn't meet many new people these days and didn't have a speech prepared about my blindness. I needed to get something ready, I guessed. I extended my hand in the direction of Mrs. Hightower's voice and heard a click of heels on the floor. Her hand was warm in mine. She had probably just gotten out of a heated car.

"Lovely to meet you, Mrs. Moody. I've seen your show on the computer."

In taking a hand, I would usually have a sense of someone by now, but nothing came through. Only the sense that someone with warm hands was nervously pumping my arm. "Let's go sit in the library and talk. I have a few questions for you, Mrs. Hightower, so I hope you won't mind providing some answers."

"If I have them," the woman said from behind me.

We'd spoken briefly on the phone about the history of the house and I'd lured her here knowing she loved history, but what I really wanted to ask about was Belinda McMahon and her ghost.

We sat in the leather chairs by the fireplace, a spot I was becoming familiar with. The fire was still burning from earlier and my shins warmed in the heat.

"Eve, can you fix us a cup of tea? Is that preferable or would you like a cup of coffee, Mrs. Hightower?"

"Tea is fine and please call me Joan." Her perfume was heavy and spicy.

I pretended to look towards the fire and wondered if I'd hit my mark. I still wasn't sure if looking off into space looked freaky and made people feel uncomfortable. I was wondering what question to lead with when Joan spoke.

"I haven't been in this house for a month or two. I see you haven't done anything to it yet."

I detected a nervous quality in her words like she might be lying. That wasn't telepathy, but simple intuition. "No. We just got here, really. I doubt we'll change much except the sheets."

Joan chuckled nervously, and I pictured her studying me.

"As you can imagine, I'm very curious why Belinda McMahon wanted me to have this house. I hope you can provide an answer to that."

"Didn't you get a letter from her?" Joan's voice went higher, like she was only trying out a scary question.

"Yes, I did get a letter to say she hoped someone with my talent could help. Did you read the letter?"

"No, I only knew there was a letter."

She was lying. I nodded, then waited for answers.

Finally, Joan sighed. "Like she said, Belinda wanted you to investigate this house."

"Because she was a fan of the show?"

"Yes. She admired your ability with spirits and watched your show regularly. We both are fans, were fans. Belinda watched your episodes over and over. She thought you had wonderful onscreen presence as well as an uncanny ability and sensitivity to ghosts."

I couldn't tell Belinda's friend that I'd lost the whole reason I'd inherited the house, even if I desperately hoped my lack of telepathy was only temporary. I needed to know more from this woman, so I continued without divulging I was a fake. "And this wonderful old place has a ghost she wanted me to help."

"Yes." She almost whispered.

"What does the ghost need, do you know?"

"No." Her answer came too quickly for honesty.

"You can't tell me, or you don't know?"

"I don't know," she said, her voice a least two registers higher than five sentences ago.

Eve's footsteps on the floor interrupted my interrogation of our guest. I assumed Eve was balancing a tea tray by the slowness of her steps approaching.

"Here we go," Eve said. The tray was set on a table near us and I heard the slosh of tea being poured.

"Joan was just telling me that she knew Belinda wrote me a letter." I tried not to say it accusingly, already sensing I might have gone too far with this skittish woman.

I heard Eve hand a cup to Joan, a "thank you" then Joan stirred her tea, the spoon hitting the sides of the cup. The tinkling sounded like Eve had broken out real tea cups and saucers. Then my tea was handed to me in a mug and I was slightly disappointed, like I'd been forced to drink from a sippy cup instead of a real cup. Even though I knew the fewer moving parts on anything for me the better, it still left me with a twinge of sadness. At Harry's funeral, my mother had chastised Eve about not handing me hot tea in a cup and saucer, and now Eve was being very careful.

"Belinda must have been an interesting person. Did she not have family to leave the house to?"

Eve pulled a chair into the group and I heard the creak of the chair springs as she sat.

"She has an estranged daughter living in Florida."

I thought about how I'd feel if my mother gave the family house to a stranger. "Was Belinda tempted to leave Cove House to her?"

"Not at all. Her daughter thought she was crazy and tried to have Belinda put away in a home fifteen years ago. This was when her mother said there was a spirit in the house."

That explained something. "How long did Belinda live here," I asked.

From the next room, Carlos yelled "watch out!" and then there was a crashing sound in the foyer. Not enough noise to be the whole chandelier.

"I'll be right back," Eve said as she left the room, her footsteps tapping across the floor.

"Belinda inherited this house from her grandfather at the age of thirty-five but didn't move here until after her daughter had set out on her own and moved to Florida. Belinda was here about forty years."

"And you knew her all that time?"

"Mercy no. I moved to Smugglers' Cove about five years ago to be closer to my son and his family and met Belinda through the historical society."

I heard a swallow of tea.

I wanted Mrs. Hightower to understand how seriously I took the task I now had to find and help this ghost. Even if Eve was the one I had to work through. "I will do everything I possibly can to contact this lingering spirit and see what help I can be."

"That's what Belinda hoped."

"Our investigation starts tonight. I believe the ghost was murdered in a bedroom upstairs." I decided to throw it all out there. "Can you confirm this?"

Eve returned and put a log on the fire while explaining that the electrician's tool box fell and spilled.

"It was a bit mysterious. That thing weighs twenty pounds and wasn't sitting on the edge of anything."

I made a note to ask Carlos about it later. Could a ghost tip over such a weight?

"The electrician was spooked and left and now Carlos is measuring levels around the area," Eve said settling back into the chair. "I'm pretty sure Carlos said something to scare him off, social pariah that he is. Probably said it was the house ghost."

Joan's tea cup met the saucer with a clink and I heard enough to realize she was standing.

"I must get back to the museum. It's been lovely talking with you."

I quickly placed my mug on the table beside my armchair. I had hoped for more from this woman and wondered why she came if she was going to deny knowing anything about the ghost. "It's been lovely talking with you, too," I said. "Do you want to stay informed on what we find?" I stood, knowing that was the polite thing to do when your guest is about to make a mad dash to the door.

"I'm sure I'll see it on your show." She cleared her throat, possibly to get her voice down to a comfortable octave.

"Please don't leave on my account," Eve said from four feet away. "I didn't mean to interrupt your conversation." My cousin sounded regretful, not realizing that this woman was guarding something she did not want to give up. Not even to me.

"Oh, no," Joan said. "I have to head back."

I wasn't getting psychic signals of a lie, but I was sure Eve was. "I hope we can keep in touch. You're the only local person we know here." I tried to not sound desperate as I extended my hand for hers.

"That would be lovely. Thank you for the tea." Joan Hightower's footsteps clicked across the floor, Eve's footsteps close by. She hadn't seen my extended hand.

"Joan?" I called. I had to ask. "Before you leave, is there anything at all that you can tell me about this ghost. Who she was, what she wants?" I turned towards them, now knowing I must've looked strange speaking to Joan, but facing the fire. There was a pause.

"There is one thing I know. The ghost is not a woman, but a man."

I stopped and held my breath, like waiting for wildlife to feed from your hand. "Are you sure?"

"Oh yes. That I'm sure of. And if I recall Belinda's words correctly, he's quite a handsome man."

Footsteps tapped their way to the door and Joan Hightower was gone.

CHAPTER 8

Eve and I walked along the grass in front of what she'd just called "the big curvy window," my arm in hers, like most blind people do to insure they don't step off a fifty-foot cliff.

When I suggested we take a walk outside now that the rain had let up, Eve had groaned but relented. She could probably see what a gray day awaited us, but I needed fresh air.

It was only since working with me that Eve had discovered she'd inherited the family gift in a small way. Recently, I'd helped her rein in her flailing psychic abilities that were making her life miserable, something she'd attributed to her crazy personality. I'd known better. Eve had been plagued with accurate hunches and severely accurate intuition for the last few years and hadn't known that it was more than that. It was the Primrose blessing or curse, whatever way you wanted to look at it. I loved my little cousin with a fierceness I'd never felt for anyone else.

"Thanks for coming out here in this wind tunnel," I joked, my hair whipping around on my head.

"No problem, Boss Lady," she said.

I really was grateful, but I had to stop thanking her for helping me. For one thing, it's her job now. I pay her well to describe the ocean as an "angry field of white waves, all the way to the sky edge," and for another thing, it's getting old saying, "Have I said, 'thank you' today?" I know Eve is getting sick of my gratefulness, but I hoped she wasn't getting tired of my neediness.

"The edge of the cliff goes out on either side of the property, in a U, making a little cove down below," Eve said.

"How far out?"

"On the left side, the length of five Floatvilles and on the right side, a little less, making the cove opening face north slightly."

That was easy to imagine.

"There's a path leading down to the ocean, it looks like," Eve said, turning our direction. The sun had come out and feeling the warmth on my face was like a kiss. My eyes were open, presumably staring up at the big ball of a sun, but I saw nothing aside from the darkness. I'd thought about just keeping my eyes closed like lots of other blind people who say it's more work to keep them open. I wasn't ready to give up on the world yet and had chosen to keep them open, make that extra muscular effort, just in case. Especially since the Roslyn restaurant where I saw the room and a ghost, something that wouldn't have happened if my eyes were closed.

"Tell me how you know there's a path."

"The cliff edge has a wooden fence that doesn't look strong enough to prevent much from bursting through. One of those old-time western rail fences with diagonal . . .thingies."

I laughed. "Posts. I got it."

The word thingies came up a lot with Eve.

"There's a break in the fence, a gate and a sandy path that leads down. There's a railing that's painted green, made from lumber, and it looks like it's fairly new."

We walked a few steps and stopped.

"Then stairs begin. Stairs made from flat rocks," Eve said.

The wind tossed my hair towards my face, not yet long enough to be annoying. I imagined Eve's long black hair was dancing around her shoulders unless she'd tied it back. I'd brought teal-colored hair dye to Oregon and fully intended to ask Eve to get my hair back to its Moody color. Maybe tomorrow.

"The stairs switchback in a zigzag. I'd say from the top to the beach below is as tall as a three-story apartment building. I can't see the beach, so it must be small. Wait here," she said, and unhooked her arm.

I breathed deeply and took in the taste and scent of the briny air. My imagination had to be good enough for now as I thought of the sea of whitecaps as far as Eve could see.

"It's a small pebbly beach, looks like," Eve said, returning and putting my arm through hers again. "Probably forty feet long and only twenty feet from the foot of the stairs to the water."

I was a swimmer and had always loved the water. I hadn't thought about whether blind people could swim or not. I'd have to look that up online. I doubted I'd be able to scuba dive again, as a blind person, but maybe this summer I'd get in that water. Certainly, I could wade in the ocean at the very least, walk that beach.

"Is the tide in or out?" I asked.

"I don't know. I'll check."

I could feel her extract what I imagined to be her phone and within seconds she had her answer.

"Almost fully out. Low tide is at two p.m., and it's just past noon."

I had an amusing thought. "Stevens, who was jailed for smuggling, buys a house with a small beach and high cliffs on either side. Pretty good spot to bring goods in and out, wouldn't you say?"

Eve agreed.

"I wonder if this is the cove the town is named after. Do you see the coastline in either direction? Are there other coves?"

"Not that I can see," she said. "The cliffs extend north for a bit and to the south, the height of the cliff drops off gradually."

I'd ask Joan Hightower about the name Smuggler's Cove next time I saw her. Did I own the frontage too? If so, Belinda McMahon's gift was more generous than I'd originally thought.

Surely, Joan Hightower would have information about the cove, something she could pass along to me. At the very least I hoped she'd be comfortable telling me how the town of Smuggler's Cove got its name.

***

Seated around the lunch table, Carlos, Eve, and I talked about what we knew so far. One woman had died in a bedroom on the second floor, one man was elusive, and a heavy tool kit had tipped over. I was finally ready to tell them about the moving coffee cup from that morning. Once I'd recounted the story, Carlos ran off for equipment to take readings in the kitchen even though it was far too late for anything to still linger.

Eve also jumped up, excited that something paranormal had finally happened with me. "That's amazeballs," she said, heading to the sink.

"I have no idea what coffee cups I used," I said.

"I'm touching all the cups in the sink," she said. "I don't feel anything."

"Imagine yourself opening a big gate to let everything in," I said trying to teach her to tune into the receiving end and let the messages come through. That was what we'd been working on before the accident— her openness to receive messages. Her talent was coming along nicely but I felt badly that she'd recently been under pressure to speed up her learning curve with urgency that hadn't been there months ago.

"Do you think it was Harry who moved the mug?" Carlos asked.

"I don't know. I'd like to think so but . . ." I didn't know what else to say. I'd hoped with all my heart it was Harry seeing I'd been talking about him to whomever had been listening. I'd specifically asked for a sign.

While eating chicken salad sandwiches with grapes and celery, and salty potato chips, we talked about the occurrences in the house and if there were two ghosts. I still hadn't told them that I'd seen an apparition in the Roslyn Eatery. I wasn't sure why I kept that a secret, but it was such an amazing tidbit of good news that I savored it privately until I decided what it meant.

Since seeing inside that restaurant, there hadn't been a repeated occurrence of sight. No rooms, no tables and chairs, no pirate-looking apparition scurrying around a corner. Although the investigation at Cove House was exciting, I also looked forward to getting back to the Roslyn restaurant to see if that ghost appeared again. Unfortunately, Jim had been spooked when the ghost touched him, and so far, he hadn't given us a second date to continue the investigation. I was sure I could convince him to let us back in. Pinching was not good for business.

"Good sandwiches, Eve." I'd buttered the bread and cut the finished products, contributing somewhat to putting lunch together and handling a knife finally, even though it was a dull knife with a rounded edge.

"I'll be glad when you can cook again, Bryn. I can stop taking those botulism meds!" Carlos laughed.

It was a running joke that Eve couldn't cook, was terrible at the domestic arts, and Carlos wasn't much better. They'd lived together briefly, trying to save money on rent and I'd always imagined their apartment full of fast food wrappers, laundry, and dust balls.

While talking about everything we knew about the strangeness of Cove House, my team and I agreed there might be more than one ghost. Even though there'd been paranormal action in the kitchen, we still planned to begin our investigation in the bloody bedroom.

"My interaction in here was much different from what Eve felt in the bedroom," I said. "If it's the same ghost, she probably showed Eve so much for a reason. I just got a moved coffee cup."

"She brushed my shoulder," Eve added, her mouth full. "That freaked me out."

"I got great levels in the bedroom, too," Carlos said. "And the blood on the wall is sexier for our show than a coffee cup moving. Unless we catch the mug that reads, 'Witchy Woman' when it's levitating."

"Is there a 'Witchy Woman' mug?" I asked, making a note that Mrs. McMahon might have thought of herself as a witch.

"All the mugs are theme," Eve answered. "One's got a photo of Captain Jack Sparrow, one has an inspirational quote about never giving up, another reads, 'I Heart Sailors,' another is from the museum in town."

"Speaking of witchy, I want to start at one a.m. tonight." Between one and three is when we always got the best results due to fewer disturbances in the atmosphere with most people sleeping, checked out, down for the count. Ghosts like privacy. Or ghosts needed privacy to come through. Less electrical disturbance.

I hadn't decided yet which one.

"You got it, Boss," Carlos said. "Let's find this ghost and get some EVP on tape."

***

As is usually the case when we do what I call a summoning, I rest before. Even though I might not pull in anything tonight, I also might, and I'd decided to get some shut eye before we started. Contacting ghosts typically takes a lot out of me and I often end up exhausted after the investigation. I've been known to sleep in the van on the way home from the job, like some coddled rock star or athlete.

Hoping to summon this ghost, I went to my room to close my eyes at 8:00 p.m. with my phone alarm set for 11:45. Eve was to check on me at midnight. I'd dress in what Carlos called a Moody vestidos and we'd begin filming in the bedroom with the mural and the blood.

But, I woke before the alarm went off and had a feeling that something was happening in my room. I wasn't sure I was being psychic, but the creepy feeling of someone staring at me, crept across my sensibilities like a chiffon scarf in a breeze. Had I dreamed that someone was watching me? I was a prolific dreamer but didn't remember what I'd been dreaming just now.

"Hello?" I said, sitting up in the bed, remembering I was still wearing a sweatshirt and yoga pants. My phone told me it was 11:15. I had another half hour to sleep. Instead, I swung my legs out of bed and slipped into my boots. Things like turning on lights, no longer mattered to me as I headed for where I knew the door to be.

I found the door knob, opened the door and started out to the hall. Voices drifted up the staircase from below. Familiar voices. It sounded like Carlos and Eve were in the kitchen talking and thanks to my amazing new hearing I heard every word.

"She could have killed us all if she'd lit the match and the fire caught and spread out like it was going to. What if I hadn't been there?" Eve's voice was full of worry.

"But she didn't light the match. We just need to make sure she knows matches are not on her to-do list." Carlos sounded like he was walking around the kitchen.

Eve said something quietly and they laughed.

I took a deep breath to calm my racing heart. I was a burden. That was a given. I knew that already, but hearing them talk about me like this in the kitchen, like I'm a child who can't be trusted, was disappointing. Not disappointing because I thought Eve and Carlos were better than talking about me behind my back. This had nothing to do with petty feelings.

I was disappointed that I'd put these two in the position of worrying that I'd burn the house down with my need to participate in everyday activities. My chin dropped to my chest before I realized it. I lifted my head trying not to give in to self-pity, and as I did, I heard a noise above me. Higher than the ceiling. Up the staircase on the third floor, I believed.

I remembered counting out twenty steps to the staircase from my bedroom door and as I moved to find the wall with my hand, I had a clear flash of what I imagined the stairs to look like. I moved along the hall to where the staircase was and when I reached the banister I heard the noise again. It was a squishing sound, now on the stairs, a sound that I could not place. I had no guess as to what could be squishing at the top of the stairs to the third floor.

There was a moment when I thought about going back to my room to wait for Eve to wake me and pretend I hadn't woken early. No. I started up the stairs. If I remembered correctly, there were eleven stairs in one direction, a landing of six of my steps to the right and eleven stairs to the third floor. I was correct.

I stood at the top of the staircase, listening, breathing lightly.

"Is anyone there?" I asked.

I walked away from the top of the stairs, taking note of how many steps I'd taken, like leaving a breadcrumb trail in the forest to get home. "I mean you no harm. Do you live in this house?"

I heard the squish again, this time closer. Maybe only a few feet away.

The blackness in front of my face seemed to fade to gray and I gasped. A wavy shadow crossed in front of my vision. Yes, vision. Like at the Roslyn Eatery, I could see something. A moving apparition to the right, then more light crept into the picture in front of me, spreading to the edges and when I saw a lamp in the distance, I almost cried out loud.

I walked towards the light, slowly. "I can see," I whispered in disbelief.

The lamp sat on a long table between two wooden chairs upholstered in red and gold striped fabric. I reached out to touch the table and laughed. "What's happening?" If this was only a dream, it was a cruel trick, one in which I'd wake only to go to the third floor to feel around looking for a table, lamp and two chairs in my blindness. I turned at another sound by the stairs to see a marmalade tabby cat run down the hall and duck into a room. At the doorway to that room, a figure stood, watching me.

"Who are you?" I asked.

The shadowy figure straightened and backed into the room quickly, leaving me.

"No, don't go. I'm…"

I moved forward, heading towards the doorway twenty feet away, but by the time I'd taken a few steps I'd gone blind again and bumped into something.

Darkness had set in.

"Please. Come back," I said to the inky blackness in front of me.

***

I stood at the top of the staircase on the second floor, wondering if my surroundings were similar to what I'd seen on the third floor.

The camera was rolling, and I was staring straight ahead, talking to my show's subscribers, people I called Mood Peeps.

"What we know so far, and, understand that this will be an ongoing investigation, is that the house was once inhabited by a smuggler. The owner of Cove House was jailed for unethical shipping practices. We suspect that one, probably two, and who knows how many more people have died within these walls."

For tonight's investigation, I'd worn my favorite red pleather jacket, black jeans with studs, a black turtleneck and loads of silver jewelry. My dark, edgy look. I hadn't dyed my hair yet, so I wore a black fedora that Eve said looked "fetching" and covered up the fact my trademark hair wasn't camera ready. I'd get to the teal dye tomorrow.

"My sources tell me there is mystery surrounding the history of this grand old Queen Anne mansion. Suspicious history, that involves murder and smuggling. This is going to be one creepy investigation, Mood Peeps. Let's get to it, shall we? Carlos, turn out the lights and let's get freaked out."

"And cut," Carlos said. "That looked like you were talking directly into the camera. I only had to adjust a tiny bit in the middle to follow your eyeline."

"Awesome job, Moody. She's baaaaaack," Eve said in a sing-songy voice, taking my arm to move me a few steps.

I hadn't told either of them about seeing the shadowy ghost on the third floor. Not yet. They'd both made such a big deal about the coffee cup that I wanted to wait. But, I was sure tonight's spring in my step and underlying grin was because of seeing a ghost earlier. And the third-floor landing. I'd seen everything up here, including one of the coach house cats.

As we moved to the bloody bedroom down the hall, I told them I'd heard a meow and asked if anyone had seen a cat inside the house.

"Great Googly Mooglies," Carlos said, his favorite expression now instead of swearing.

Carlos' terror of cats often made his mother laugh to think her son had no problem encountering a ghost but ran when he saw a cat.

"Maybe one of the property cats got in," Eve said, moving my position for the camera.

"Am I beside where you saw the blood?" I asked.

Eve took my hands and placed them on the wall. "Right here. Feel anything?"

I closed my eyes, trying to empty my mind. All I could think about was the cat and the shadowy figure by the door. "Not yet." At least I sounded hopeful that something was possible.

"That's the spirit," Eve said. It was a favorite phrase of hers and Carlos always laughed, repeating the word 'Spirit.'"

"Keep your eyes open for a cat."

I heard Carlos say a real swear word under his breath and imagined him setting up the shot from behind our very expensive movie camera with a look of fear on his face and chill in his heart about a ten-pound house pet.

"Does my hat still look good?" I asked Eve, my hair, makeup, and wardrobe person now that I couldn't be relied on to make good choices on the visual.

She made an adjustment on the fedora, applied a touch of lip gloss and moved away, probably to where she always stood when I filmed on-camera segments, which was behind Carlos' right shoulder, so that she could see the camera's viewfinder.

"Ready when you are," Carlos said.

I looked to where I imagined the camera to be located, and when Carlos complimented me on my accuracy, I began the next segment of our show.

"We are in one of eight bedroom suites in Cove House. It was here only a few days ago I saw blood on the wall right behind me. It was also here the presence of a woman was felt. We believe that she died from an injury in this exact spot. The blood started at what I estimated to be her heart level and slid to the ground, like she'd been skewered with a sword, fell against the wall and slid to the floor." I motioned to the wall behind me, and before I could continue, Carlos spoke.

"Holy hell. It's on camera. The blood."

I turned to the wall, as if to look at the blood. "And there it is," I lied. "I'm assuming if you can see it on camera, Carlos, Mood Peeps will see it too." I tried to not sound disappointed though truthfully, I was the only person who couldn't see the blood. Now, anyone with eyesight and the internet could see what I couldn't. "You're still seeing it through the camera, Carlos?"

"It's faint but yes, there's definitely something on the wall. Wouldn't you say, Eve?"

Eve concurred. "I see it too, but only in the camera, not with my bare eyes."

I couldn't turn back to face the camera because I didn't know where the camera was any more. It was better for me to look way off the mark, like I wasn't even trying, than to focus just inches from the eye of the camera. Still, I did not want to interrupt this moment of discovery. Having blood seen on camera would go up there with our viral video that catapulted my show into fame last year. I put my hands on the wall, hopefully near the blood, closed my eyes and drew in a deep breath. I thought about editing, instead of thinking of ghosts and wondered how to make a good transition to the next shot, which just seemed wrong considering we had something mind blowing in front of us--trailing blood down a mural of what appeared to be a painting of this house.

"Carlos, can you see it? The blood?

"Only on camera, Moody."

I turned to where I thought the camera was, kept my head low, like I was thinking and spoke. "Are you here with us, tonight?" I waited. "We are in this house to help you. Can you give us a sign?"

Eve interrupted. "She wants to come through but can't."

I nodded. "She can't," I repeated like the shyster I was. Shoot. Eve was getting something, and I was a plain and simple con artist pretending I got the feelings, too. A part of me wanted to go back to my bedroom, lie down, and cry. Being a good sport was getting harder and harder now that Eve had the ability to do what I used to do. Then I remembered I had to finish this segment and stop feeling sorry for myself. "Can you tap the window, touch one of us, or move something?" I said to the female spirit Eve felt. "Maybe speak your name."

We waited while the tape rolled. It was normal to get nothing. What was exceptional were those tiny moments when something got through. Lately, we'd had more ghost action than we'd had all last year. Even in this house, our action had been phenomenal. We often taped hours of nothing, hours of me asking for a sign, hours of waiting.

"Eve? Are you feeling emotion from the spirit?" I remembered she'd felt something last time.

"Like you, Moody, I feel anger."

Ah, she was angry. "I believe our ghost died right here, at the hands of someone she hated. What a great find, this house is. Our very own ghost to investigate." My blood quickened, and I had to remind myself to calm down. "Gone too soon. Who was this ghost? A smuggler? The wife of a smuggler? The house's history is rich with suspense. This investigation is not over." I chuckled like this was the best case I'd ever been on. "Moody out." I said. "For now."

"And cut," Carlos said.

I leaned against the wall wondering if we got what we needed. At this point, I always went behind the camera to watch the playback.

"Bryn, please tell me you saw the blood," Eve said. "Or felt the ghost.

"Nope. Tell me what you felt, Eve." I waited.

"Mostly hatred and anger at the person who killed her." Eve was walking around the room now. "I didn't get a feeling of who she is or what time period she came from, but she was furious."

"And the blood?" I asked. "You could only see it on camera? Not with your eyes?"

"Right."

I wasn't sure what to make of what had just happened but whatever it was, it was rich. At least one of us was getting something, enough to make a great show. "Carlos, do you want me to sit with you while you splice and edit tonight? You could describe to me what you're seeing." I'd always accompanied him to decide on what would make up the show.

"I think I got it," he said.

As the director of the show, I usually sat to Carlos' left, listening to our playbacks, searching the footage for anomalies. But not tonight. I could slump in a chair near Carlos' work station in the den and wait for him to tell me what he found. But it wouldn't be the same and I was pretty sure my tech guy could pull everything off our data that was show-worthy and present it to me verbally after I'd had a good night's sleep.

We made a plan to convene in the den at eight tomorrow morning, take a look at the edited episode Carlos would be doctoring all night. I'd be listening, and Eve would be describing what the footage looked like.

Even though it would be a farce about me seeing the blood, and feeling the ghost, I couldn't be too hard on myself. I had seen a ghost tonight. But my ghost was not a woman who couldn't get through. My ghost got through loud and clear.

Almost reluctantly, it seemed.

CHAPTER 9

Smuggler's Cove Museum was described to me as a fake log cabin off the very small main street of a rickety-looking coastal town.

"How many blocks is the downtown?" I asked, as Carlos parked The Marshmallow near the museum.

"Three solid blocks of stores, then a gas station, it looks like." Eve sounded like she'd never seen such a small town before. She didn't like living in the boonies and probably couldn't wait to get back to traffic and skyscrapers.

"Is there a sign outside the museum?" I asked, needing to keep the narrative going.

Carlos took this one. "There's a wooden sign with old font saying Smuggler's Cove Museum, with an anchor after the last word. As a matter of fact, there's mucho stuff in town with anchors. Must be part of their logo in Smuggler's Cove."

"And Mrs. Hightower has put up the OPEN sign, to welcome us in," Eve said, facetiously.

We walked in the front door, a bell jingling our arrival. I heard voices, a hushed conversation off to the right, and immediately recognized Joan's distinctively high-pitched voice.

"There she is now," Joan said, probably forgetting that I'm blind, not deaf. I imagined she meant me, the way she cut herself off.

We'd made the five-mile trip to town to secure our tenuous relationship with the only person we knew in Oregon, a woman who'd also run out of the house yesterday, afraid to divulge what she knew. Joan's reaction to me or us hadn't been normal, and I intended to get to the bottom of her skittishness.

"Mrs. Hightower," Eve said, "We thought we'd visit your museum."

Eve sounded credible.

Heels tapped on the floor, getting closer. I put out my hand. "Hello again, Joan." I felt her warm hand in mine as she attempted one of her pumping handshakes.

"Mrs. Moody, nice to see you again."

I heard footsteps on the other side of the room. Whoever Joan had been speaking with when we arrived, they'd moved off. "If you have guests to attend to, don't let us keep you," I offered. I hadn't thought we might compete with others for the museum curator's attention right after the place opened for the day.

"Oh, that's fine. They're my friends who just dropped in to say hello. We have a new display of arrowheads and they are looking at those. What can I do for you?"

I couldn't say we dropped in to look at arrowheads because I couldn't see the dang arrowheads. The wonders of the Smuggler's Cove museum were lost on me unless Eve described the things I assumed were in glass cases. Even then, so much would be lost in the translation. I intended to get right to the point. "As a psychic," I said, "I know things when other people don't." I paused for effect. "Yesterday, I sensed that you weren't telling me something and I hoped we might have another chat. I'd like to put your mind at rest about our investigation, and our intentions."

I wished I could look deep into her eyes to fix her with one of my stares, but instead, I just waited, my gaze fixed in the darkness in front of me, listening, even smelling her spicy perfume.

"Please follow me," she said.

Eve took my arm and led me to another room where I was guided to sit in a hard, wooden chair with arm rests. "I can leave you two," Eve said.

"That sounds fine," Joan said, her voice lower than I'd ever heard. "We'll be only five minutes."

I waited to hear what this mysterious woman had to tell me that couldn't be said in front of anyone else. Papers shuffled on what I assumed was a desk.

Finally. "You're right. I have secrets. But it's in your best interest I not reveal anything. Not yet." Her voice was no longer frivolous but determined and almost foreboding.

"When can I expect full disclosure, Joan? I'm trying to unravel a mystery here." What was this woman keeping from me?

"I'm waiting to see what you turn up in the house. Your investigation. I want you to go into this with a clear mind, no expectations."

What the hell did that mean? "It might help if you could give me a hint of what I'm looking for. I don't want to say I'm flying blind but it's kind of feeling that way."

"I'm sorry. I can only tell you to find Belinda's ghost. Someone who is not the murdered woman in the bedroom, but a man."

"Is he looking for something? Is that why he lingers?"

The woman sitting across from me was silent and I wanted badly to read her expression, or at least have Eve present to read her expression. "Does he wear boots? I thought I heard boots on the third floor."

"Yes, I believe he might wear boots."

"What time period is he from?"

"I'm not sure."

"Maybe from a time when men wore coattails and boots?"

"Maybe."

I decided to try to draw out more by playing the sympathy card. "What if I never find this ghost? What if he doesn't appear for me, like he did for Belinda?"

"Oh, he'll appear. He's quite full of himself."

Aha. "He likes attention?"

"I need to get back to the museum now." Her chair scraped against the floor.

I heard Joan leave the room, speak to Eve in a low tone and I waited. I stood and thought about what I'd learned in the last two minutes. Even though I felt slightly triumphant at getting more information from the museum curator, I hated being this helpless.

But more than that, I hated hearing a juicy tidbit from someone about a ghost and then not being able to read her expression.

***

Dinner that night was ruined by a call from my mother. It wasn't what she said but just the sound of her voice that made me lose my appetite. She called just as I was shoving a wrap with Smuggler's Cove Delicious Deli chicken and Caesar salad into my mouth.

"Ron says they are investigating Mrs. Giovanni's death. So there."

I put the wrap down on my plate. "Congratulations. Maybe you can contact ghosts after all."

"I just had a feeling and Eve confirmed it."

Dig.

"I'm glad. Eve is a huge help to me as well, these days."

"Ron would like to meet you."

I smiled. "Isn't it early for your boyfriend to meet the family, Rachel? How long have you been dating?"

"It's not that. I told him you'd seen Terri drinking poison."

My mother had lied to her cop boyfriend. "If I meet him I'll have to call you out on that one." I put her on speaker so the other two could enjoy what I went through.

"You'll do no such thing, young lady. I won't have you call me a liar. I did what I had to do to get Terri's murder avenged."

"We're just about to eat dinner. Can I call you back?" This was my own standby phrase that meant,

"How about we drop this subject and I'll pretend you didn't call."

"No need. I just wanted to find out what the weather is like over there and if I should pack my rain slicker."

Carlos chuckled. Damn him.

"Yes, it's rainy here but you aren't exterminating for another few days, right? We're heading back to Seattle tomorrow." I had to be firm with my mother before she showed up at the door with a giant suitcase and Ron, both looking for a month's vacation on the Oregon coast.

"I was able to get the exterminator to come early, so I need to get out tomorrow."

I counted to three, calmly. "Where will you go tomorrow?"

"I'll drive to Oregon, of course."

"We leave here tomorrow."

"I can stay in a house all by myself. I don't need you, Bryndle. Except to give me the address and a key."

"I'll call you later," I said and hung up.

I wondered what Carlos and Eve's faces looked like as I counted to ten this time. "Don't anyone give that woman the address."

***

The evening's investigation was to be conducted on the third floor this time. The woman who died on the second floor was now of lesser interest to me for obvious reasons. I couldn't reach her. She wasn't my ghost. She didn't allow me anything unless she was the ghost who moved my coffee cup, but I hadn't been able to get anything in the kitchen since.

The third-floor ghost, who I believed was a handsome man in boots, seemed to have an uncanny effect on me--an ability that allowed me to see him. In his presence, I'd seen everything, including the lamp, the rug, him. The strange twist was that I was starting to think it was not sight from my eyes, but psychic sight. What I saw in front of my face was inside my head, not coming from my useless eyes. Still, what I sensed in front of me was actually there. My mind had shown me a banister, then I reached out and saw my hand touching the banister. So, although my eyes were still useless, I could see in the presence of this ghost.

Very strange, indeed.

Carlos had put together a compelling piece of footage for our next show. It was a compilation of our investigation the night before, and after I gave my okey dokey to upload it, we had ourselves a new episode of Moody Paranormal Investigations. That felt good after such a long time of using old footage.

That was the good news. The bad news was that it turned out that the blood seen on the wall was actually a smear of something on the camera lens and we weren't able to capitalize on our viewers seeing the bloody wall, like we'd thought. It was hugely disappointing, but something had already warned me that it was too good to be true. I hadn't believed what was seen on camera was the blood on the wall and it turned out my instinct, or my returning psychic abilities, had been correct.

Shortly after going live with our new episode, Eve started tweeting and posting like a social media maniac and that's when the fun started. The show was getting hits like it was the latest video of a pop star disrobing. Our subscriber numbers were increasing at such a rate that we wondered what had happened. That night, Carlos kept a running commentary about the success of the episode as we ate a baked lasagna that I happened to make all by myself.

Earlier I'd gotten the noodles, two jars of sauce, (I know it's cheating, but hey), a bag of shredded mozzarella cheese and put everything on the counter with a lasagna pan Eve found in the cupboard and had since washed, just in case. While the ground turkey was frying, I started the process of layering lasagna into the pan on top of marinara sauce. An hour in the oven and Eve helped me pull it out to rest on the counter for fifteen minutes.

"Two thousand more." Carlos announced through a mouthful of chips he'd opened just before dinner was served.

"What's happened that's getting us such coverage?" I asked.

"I'd guess we got on some site's search engine for ghosts and when someone searches, they get our link."

This was what we'd been hoping for after the ghost video a year ago that put us on Yahoo News and sent us into the stratosphere of paranormal occurrences. "We need more footage tonight and a quick upload tomorrow to keep up the momentum." The more successful our site was, the better chance of being able to continue with this YouTube show and support all three of us. Eve dished out the lasagna onto bowls, so I wouldn't push my square off a flat plate and onto the tablecloth and we sat down to eat.

I was surprised that the meal I'd made was actually quite edible. Not very unique with everything coming from bags and jars, but it was a tasty lasagna. As we ate in silence, I wondered how long I'd be able to fool the public into thinking that Moody still saw ghosts. Everything I'd said on the new show about my visions, was a lie. I was a sham.

By the time I was standing at the sink holding a sponge, my hands in the hot water, Carlos reported a jump of twenty thousand new subscribers and attributed our success to a link from Yahoo News that was titled "Oregon Ghost Hunter Finds Bloody Wall."

Eve laughed. "Now you're an Oregon ghost hunter, Bryn."

"We didn't post the smear on the lens, did we?"

"Negatory," Carlos said. "But you did say you saw a bloody wall."

"Eve saw the bloody wall," I said. "I hi-jacked her revelation."

I felt for the dish rack and put a plate in it for Eve to dry. "Eve, can you put something up on the site about us continuing the investigation tonight? It'll build excitement for when we post in a few days. Get those ghost lovers to set reminders to watch the show."

"Done and done," Eve said.

"Good," I handed Eve the next plate. "Tonight, I want to stand where I saw the shadow in the doorway. Let's get me on camera doing something for real. You guys can situate yourselves across the foyer and zoom in on me but let's not overwhelm this spirit." If this ghost was only present when I was around, I wanted to keep my awesome twosome slightly out of sight.

"Sounds bueno," Carlos said. "It might be better when you can't look directly into the camera. If your eyes are bouncing around, not hitting the lens of the camera, our distance might be a good excuse."

"Exactly." I imagined Eve shooting Carlos a look to say 'shut up' but could never be sure about these things. I placed the last dish in the rack and dried my hands on the dish towel hung over my shoulder. "Another accomplishment," I said. "I did the dishes." What I hadn't yet tried as a blind person could fill the Seattle Seahawks football stadium.

I patted Eve's shoulder in camaraderie, as I bumped against her. "Thanks for helping me do the dishes. Next stop, dying my hair teal, please and thank you." I needed Eve for stuff like this and there was no getting around it. Eve was on duty a lot these days. When Hodor graduated from service dog school, I'd be able to give Eve more freedom but until he did all his training and passed his tests, I had to rely on these two so much, including my on-screen look. Eve would always have to help me with this. Hairdressing and makeup was not something Hodor was learning in service dog school.

"I'm going to wear the camo jacket with a low-cut black top tonight," I told Eve as she led me upstairs. "I want to look slightly sexy, if you can help me achieve that look."

"I'm thinking smoky eyes and blood red lips," Eve said.

Eve was great with makeup, being a fan of anime and cosplay. Dressing up like cartoon characters at those conventions where everyone spends weeks getting their costumes to look like Japanese cartoon characters was right up Eve's alley.

As we mounted the stairs to prepare for the witching hour, I thought about what Joan had said today. Every time I saw the elusive museum curator, she let out a tiny bit more information, almost like she couldn't help herself, poor woman.

She'd revealed that Belinda's ghost is a man who's quite full of himself. If he was even slightly narcissistic, and heterosexual, I had a plan. Tonight, I would give him something extra.

A little cleavage and some alluring makeup might be just the thing to lure Belinda's evasive ghost around the doorway and out of the shadows.

CHAPTER 10

Standing at the doorway where I'd seen the ghost wearing a long coat the night before, I waited for Carlos to get the camera set up on the tripod across the foyer. I recalled the configuration of the room, the distance from the doorway to the staircase, the color of the fabric on the two chairs by the long table. After so long of nothing, I remembered everything. And after months of not seeing color or movement, it had been like a long drink of water on a hot day to have vision again. The thought that my eyes weren't sending me the picture of the room, however, was something that had kept me awake last night.

My eyesight hadn't returned.

It was my psychic sight that gave me the view of the room. It didn't feel different from eyesight except that when I closed my eyes, I still saw the room just as clearly. I knew that because I'd closed my eyes and had been shocked the image didn't go black with my peepers shut.

Lying in bed last night, thinking about this, I'd asked myself if I could have only one of my sights back, which one did I want? I could spend weeks pondering this, not that I'd been granted one wish, like a genie in a bottle. What I'd experienced last night, had kept me thinking until the wee hours of the morning. Psychic sight allowed me to see even if it was temporary, but existing as a sighted person with no telepathy would rob me of the gift that defined who I was.

I'd gotten used to helping ghosts, used to the gratefulness I felt when I made contact, used to how important my life's work felt. It wasn't about the YouTube show. That thing made it possible to afford to do the work. It was about being a helper to the trapped spirits between worlds. Spirits who were unable to rest or cross over. Some had been held prisoner for centuries and although I wasn't sure if ghosts had a sense of time, I had to think that rattling around inside the same house for hundreds of years was like a prison sentence to beings who'd once been people in this world, people with the same sensibilities as I had.

"Ready," Carlos said from across the wide hall. "Look over here." He whistled like I was a dog whose attention he sought.

I stood up straight, got my hands out of my jacket pockets and stared to where I heard the whistling. "How's my focus?"

"Perfect," Eve said, quietly.

"Are the lights on?"

"Just one lamp to your right. On the hall table. It's dim," Carlos was great with lighting, always achieving the right effect for the mood. Frankenscar had been covered in the makeup process with something Eve swore made it pretty much disappear. I hoped she was right because the makeup cost me forty dollars and I was a tightwad.

"Count me in."

"4, 3, 2 . . ."

"Moody here. This is Day Two of our ongoing investigation on the Oregon Coast. We are on the third floor of Cove House continuing our hunt in a house we believe might have multiple spirits rattling around inside these walls. Having visited the local museum today, we learned several things that might help us understand what we're up against. One, is that the ghost of the man has attitude. He is known to be attention-seeking, or full of himself as it was told to me. Of course, that makes us hopeful that we'll be able to draw him out." I wondered if Carlos was doing a head shot only, or if our viewers could see my ample cleavage. I shifted and held up two fingers. "And two, we realized that the cove in front of the house very possibly could have been used to further the smuggling efforts of the former occupant, Mr. Stevens. It's a perfect little bay to anchor a ship and send goods to the beach. Watch this." I waited three seconds, until Carlos yelled "cut." I scratched my nose, something I'd been meaning to do for twenty long seconds. This was where we'd cut to footage of the coastline.

"Looked good," Eve said. "Want to try another one?"

We often did two versions, just in case. "Sure." I readied myself.

"4, 3, 2…"

"It's after midnight and we're on the third floor of Cove House, in an ongoing investigation of this old mansion we know has at least one ghost, if not more. Last night I heard footsteps on the third floor, where we are now. Boot steps. Of a heavy man, walking quickly. Carlos has checked to find no one else here, unless you want to include a cat who was seen roaming the house yesterday. The steps heard came from this part of the long hall. Today, we learned more about the man who owned this house after the original owners. He was operating on the wrong side of the law. Our source tells us when he returned from his jail sentence, he mysteriously disappeared. Maybe he's still wandering around inside the house. Tonight, we will try to summon him. Mood Peeps. Grab the edge of your seats. Carlos, cut the lights. Mood Peeps, prepare to be freaked out."

We often watched the playbacks and decided how much information to give out at a time. In the first version, I didn't mention the cat. The second version I decided to reveal there was a cat roaming the house to build tension, even though it had nothing to do with our ghost.

Next up, was Eve who was starting to film on-camera spots at my insistence. Eventually, I was going to have to reveal to our viewers that I'd gone blind and when that happened it could only help to have Eve ready to be my on-camera eyes. She'd tell our audience what she saw, something I could no longer do.

"Eve? Are you ready for your walk down the hall?"

I heard her footsteps coming towards me. "Ready as I'll ever be." Her voice wavered.

"Just keep it simple, like you're explaining to me." I threw that out there, although she already knew this.

From my perch in the doorway, I listened to what I believed to be Carlos setting up Eve's shot. "Eve? Just walk towards the camera and let Carlos enter first, then you."

"I'll back in and you stay about eight feet away. Ready?" Carlos asked.

"Ready," Eve said.

"4, 3, 2 . . ."

"The rooms up here on the third floor look like they've been shut up and unused for a long time." Eve sighed. "Wait, Carlos. Can we do that again?"

I heard shuffling.

"4, 3, 2. . ."

"The third floor hasn't seen much attention in the last few years, it looks like, not of the living kind, anyhow. The rooms up here are empty of furniture, except for this one with a desk. Moody says the third floor used to be servant quarters mostly. There's even a widow's walk on the roof, although we haven't been up there yet."

Their voices drifted off as they entered the room down the hall. In the next bit, I'd be in the room, but I couldn't be on film right now, shuffling blindly behind Eve, then feeling my way into a room. I heard Eve say, "retake please." Poor Eve. She did not like being on camera.

While waiting, my vision lightened slightly, flickered and then I saw the dim outline of the staircase railing in front of me. The stairs were dark but partly lit by the lamp at the end of the foyer to my right. It was happening again. I blinked frantically, willing my sight to return, to speed up.

"Are you here?" I stood taller and looked around. A painting of mountains and a raging river hung over the table. As the scene took on color, my heart pounded in my ribs, so hard I thought it might break one.

Then, I felt the presence of something close, someone watching me. I moved out from the doorway, spinning around, searching the area, visually. Knowing I was looking around the hallway was incredible to me. I could see.

Eve and Carlos laughed from the room down the hall and I heard Eve say, "Take five."

It was then that I saw him, my ghost. On the stairs. He stood several steps down, facing me. He was faint at first, but within seconds the man in front of me was as clear as if a neighbor had come to say hello. Only this visitor wore a long coat, the back tails reaching the top of his cuffed boots, a shirt with a large collar, a leather vest, knickers, and was startlingly handsome with clear eyes and black facial hair.

"How is this possible?" I whispered.

He stared as if he was waiting for me to focus on him. Our eyes locked for five long seconds. Belinda was right in telling Joan he was handsome. He looked like a movie star waiting for the director to yell "Action."

"I'm blind, but I can see you." I took two careful steps forward and as I did so, the ghost tipped his head as if to say, "You're welcome."

"Who are you?"

The apparition in front of me had black hair, just past his shoulders, a trimmed beard and moustache, and his lips curled slightly as if he was finding all this very amusing. He wasn't afraid of being seen, not shy after all. The ghost wanted me to see him. I had the sense this meeting was planned on his part.

"I can't believe I can see you."

Just as he opened his mouth to speak, Carlos and Eve emerged from the room down the hall, Carlos, still filming. Eve cleared the door and saw me near the stairs. "Stop, Bryn!"

The ghost turned his head, saw my companions and in one swoop, jumped over the staircase railing and disappeared. My vision disappeared with him.

"Stop!" Eve said. "You're at the top of the stairs, Bryn." Her voice wavered.

"I'm fine," I said to Eve who was now rushing towards me. I knew she was running by the quick tapping of her footsteps getting louder. Not because I could see her. Not anymore. The ghost was gone, and I was once again blind. "Did you see him?" I asked.

"See who? We heard you talking."

"The ghost. He was on the stairs. Did you see him just now? He jumped over the railing." I wasn't sure if the tape was still rolling. "Are we filming?"

"Yes." Carlos said.

"Mood Peeps, I'm not sure if you saw what I saw but there was a man on the stairs." I didn't try to face the camera but instead, pointed to the staircase as if I still saw it. "The ghost was a man, in a period outfit, probably from the 1800's. He was slightly translucent at first, then looked more solid. When I said I could see him, he nodded." My voice was higher than usual, but my news was too exciting to not speak in a squeak on camera. "The ghost made contact. When Carlos and Eve emerged from the room down the hall, he jumped over the railing. Did you catch that on tape, Carlos?"

"We saw nothing from here except you talking to nobody on the stairs. Nada." Carlos sounded breathless.

I pretended to scan the area, not even trying to look at the camera. "In a minute I'll have Carlos play back the tape to see if the ghost is on there."

If he was, this would be the biggest discovery of a ghost ever and the thought of the tape going viral made my pulse race. "He was on the stairs, looking at me. He wore a long coat, knickers and tall boots. Let's review the tape and see if we got him." I put my hands to my head as if I couldn't believe what had just happened. "I have never seen a ghost so clearly before. When I asked if he heard me, the ghost gestured like this." I turned my head to the side and dipped my chin to say you're welcome. "This is mind-boggling. Carlos. Let's get a reading on the stairs, see what our equipment says, and we'll take it from there."

As Carlos passed me, I smelled Eau Sauvage, the scent that matched Carlos' personality. Solid and exotic.

"Nada." Carlos said from the stairs. "Zero."

I assumed we were still filming. Eve might now have the camera. She knew how to hold it steady, zoom in for a closeup.

"There is no indication of any paranormal activity," Carlos said. "Or anything on the stairs."

"Impossible," I added. "He was just there."

Eve took my arm and led me back from the edge. Apparently, having a blind person near a staircase was unsettling.

"The camera is off," Eve said. "Bryn? Were you pretending to see a ghost?"

Did I sound like I was pretending? "No. I saw a man on the stairs."

"With your peepers?"

"Kind of." It was hard to explain. "I saw the stairs and I saw you come out of the room. You're wearing that jacket I gave you for your birthday and pink skinny jeans. Your hair is in pigtails, which looks very cute with the bows, by the way.

"Arigatou," Eve said. I often forgot that she spoke five languages, her favorite being Japanese.

"You were walking behind Carlos, who, by the way, needs a haircut."

"Oh, Gods," Eve said. "You are right. And you can't see now?"

"I cannot," I said, trying to keep the disappointment out of my voice. "I could be wrong, but it appears I can see in the presence of this apparition, whoever he is. And, he's shy around you two. When you stepped out of the room, he didn't disappear, but instead, ran off."

"That would indicate he's leaving of his own will, not just disappearing because he can't remain," Carlos said from half-way down the stairs.

That was true. Usually spirits tried very hard to remain and faded away.

Eve touched my arm. "We had the mic on high and heard you saying, 'I can see you.' Also, you said, 'I'm blind.'"

"That'll have to be edited out," I said, telling Carlos something he already knew.

125

"I'm not getting a reading of anything over here. No residual of anything on the stairs." Carlos sounded baffled. "Almost like this area is a dead zone. With none of the usual electro-magnetic ions in the air."

There was always some sort of reading, even if the click sounded every few seconds. I had an idea. "You two go downstairs. I'm going to try to contact our ghost again. No camera."

"Are you sure?"

"I'm sure." Eve's protectiveness was bothering me tonight and I had to keep from snapping at her.

"You didn't sign off," Carlos said. "We need to film an ending."

That was true. We hadn't done our usual sign off for the show yet. "Do I look presentable, Eve?"

I heard her approach and felt my cousin's hands fluffing my hair, fixing the collar of my jacket.

"Where should I look?"

"Look here," Carlos said. "Over here. Right here."

I looked up and assumed Carlos would adjust the camera's eye to hit my line of vision.

"Count me in," I said to Carlos.

"4, 3, 2 . . ."

"This has been quite a night. It isn't even 2 a.m. and we've had such a huge blast of paranormal activity that our minds are spinning, and our camera is buzzing. The spirit I saw just now did not want to remain when Carlos, the camera, and Eve arrived. He jumped over the banister, not fading away like ghosts usually do, but exiting. There were a few seconds when the others might have seen him, but they were looking at me and by the time they looked to the stairs, he was gone. I'm going to remain here on the house's third floor for another hour, in the dark, by myself to see if the ghost comes back. Scary? Maybe, but I have the eerie feeling this ghost needs something from me and I'm not about to turn my back on him now. Especially since we've come so far. Moody out. For now."

"And cut," Carlos said.

Eve laid her hand on my shoulder. "Shall I sit you in one of the chairs by the table?"

"Perfect. I'll phone you when I'm ready to call it a night," I said, feeling for my phone in my back pocket.

"We'll review the tape in the den while you hang out up here," Carlos said.

"Good idea," I said. "I'll just stay here for another hour or so, see if our ghost is still lurking."

"I wouldn't call him our ghost, Bryn," Eve said. "He seems to be just your ghost.

CHAPTER 12

Somewhere around 4:30 a.m., I realized that with my new vision I wanted to see what my house looked like and asked Caspian to leave the bedroom with me. "Can you do that without disappearing?" This arrangement was all so tentative, and I was painfully aware that the ghost sitting in the chair across from me might fade away at any moment and never return. There wasn't a guarantee to any of this.

"I roam these halls all night by myself and I believe I can accompany you on your tour." Caspian stood briskly like we were headed to a ball in the grand parlor. He even held out his hand to help me to my feet.

I took his hand and stood firmly. Did he expect us to hold hands all the way to the door? I let go and walked over to grab the doorknob, not having to feel for it in blindness. Like a gentleman, Caspian motioned for me to go ahead of him.

"Let's check out this house," I said stepping through the doorway.

"Check out," he said. "An interesting way to say it. I'm sure you'll be pleasantly surprised at what you see."

We left the bedroom like two friends heading off on an adventure. Maybe Caspian was lonely. Maybe the other ghosts in the house weren't enough. As long as his presence gave me sight, I was this guy's new best friend.

I walked the hall without my hand on the wall, found the staircase and together we descended the stairs, side by side to the first floor. Casting my eyes on the grandness of the front foyer once we reached the landing was exciting.

My inherited mansion was awesome. And not as in the surfer/skateboarder kind of awesome, but as in awe-inspiring. No wonder Eve and Carlos liked the place. The only thing that kept the foyer from being something from a movie set was a system of ropes and pulleys and mattresses, all in place to keep one monstrous chandelier from falling and cracking the floor as it exploded into pieces of expensive crystal. Carlos had set up enough ropes tied to high places that if the thing fell, it would not hit the floor but would be stopped somewhere just off the Italian tile at the two-foot mark, I estimated. Carlos was a DIY engineer.

"Your assistant has quite an imagination," Caspian said, pointing to the system of ropes.

"I see that." I was so interested in what Carlos was doing, I hadn't yet smiled at his ingenuity.

"She's simply amusing herself."

"Who are you talking about?" I turned to study his face, because I could.

"The woman who cut the chandelier." He sighed, his eyes turning at the corners sadly.

"Is someone trying to kill us?" I gestured towards the chandelier hanging by one wire.

"Not necessarily kill. Maybe taunt."

"Why?"

"Boredom. Jealousy. I'm not sure why Jacqueline does the spiteful things she does." Caspian continued down the stairs and I followed closely. He smelled like the color blue.

"Who is Jacqueline and are you sure she did this to the chandelier?"

"Probably. It's her style. And, she hates to be invisible and ignored." Caspian stopped close to the mattresses, just under the chandelier and I was about to warn him to move away when I realized he couldn't die twice.

I stood far enough back just in case. "Who is Jacqueline?" I asked.

"My wife."

"You're married?" I looked to his ring finger which was one of the only fingers on both his hands without a gold ring.

"On paper only. Before I died, we hadn't seen each other in a decade, but fate saw fit to send her to me in the afterlife." Caspian gestured to the door on the other side of the grand foyer. "Shall we take our tour?"

I decided to drop any more questions I had about Jacqueline. I wanted to see as much as I could quickly, in case my sight disappeared along with Caspian. We would begin our tour of a house I would commit to memory, my eyes feasting on the colors and configurations of everything I'd felt but hadn't seen yet. As we walked from room to room, Caspian wanted me to know his life, his associations, the details of the day he died, probably to give me information so I could honor my side of our deal. We talked like friends, even laughed at one point over his description of wanting to become a sea captain as a boy so he could say words like "dead ahead," and "hoist the mainsail."

The tour ended in the bloody wall room where I asked him what happened in here.

"A story for another time," he'd said wistfully.

I considered trying to keep the conversation going, but he left the room and waited for me outside the door. We talked about his ship, the Isabella, on our way back to my bedroom when suddenly, he looked concerned.

"I feel myself leaving," he said from my bedroom doorway. "Remember our deal."

Apparently, he couldn't materialize any time he wanted or stay as long as he wanted. Before he faded away, he hurriedly said that we'd continue our conversation later. "Of that, I'm sure," he said.

I didn't know the rules of his ghostmanship and wasn't even sure he knew, but this time he'd left not of his own accord.

I entered my bedroom blindly, cursing my reliance on a fleeting companion. I'd been lucky to have this much, I knew that, but still.

***

I shuffled into the kitchen before Eve and Carlos woke. I hadn't heard them moving around yet. It was before seven and too early for them. Me too, considering last night. My eyes were heavy, my mouth dry and I felt like I'd been at an all-nighter, which I kind of had, but without the alcohol. Sleep hadn't come for me after Caspian left. I hadn't tried.

In some regards, the visit from Caspian felt like a dream, but because I hadn't slept, I was able to realize my ghostly visit wasn't a dream. That, and the ring I now wore on my right index finger. I knew what it looked like even though this morning I couldn't see it. Last night I'd studied it though. Caspian had suggested we trade something as a token of good faith for our deal. He'd offered to give me one of the rings he wore on his right hand, a gold emblem of a lion on a shield. I gave him a bracelet with a ghost charm my mother had given me years before. At the time, I doubted his ring would remain when he left me, but it did. I could feel the heaviness of the gold on my right hand as I thought about Captain Cortez.

He was open but guarded in some regards and I got the hint of a quirky sense of humor that matched my own. I'd let him do most of the talking. Our conversation wasn't like a dinner party with friends, or the beginning days of a romance where you divulge your life story and find commonalities.

It was a business arrangement, but still, a frickin' miracle to be hanging out with a ghost.

I made coffee in the cold kitchen, having forgotten to set the coffee maker last night in our excitement about trying to contact the ghost on the third floor. Calling him "the ghost", now felt too unfamiliar after hours of feeling like I'd been interviewing a subject for a college paper on shipping in the 1800's. "How big was your ship?" I'd asked. "How many crew?" When

I'd asked if he was a smuggler, he'd looked solemn and shook his head.

I didn't know if he wasn't a smuggler or he wasn't talking, but when I asked again to clarify, he continued to shake his head as if to say that subject was out of bounds and then continued to detail the men who might have been out to get him.

"Did you ask Belinda to solve your murder?" I'd asked him.

He'd taken a long time to collect his thoughts before he answered, and I was glad to have sight because I saw deceit in his eyes when he answered. "Belinda was limited in her ability to help me," he said. Although our conversation flowed easily, Caspian Cortez was not about to give up all his information to help me find his body. I wondered what he was hiding.

I leaned against the kitchen counter, waiting for the Kona Gold coffee to drip, my arms crossed. The kitchen felt colder than usual, and I wondered if Jacqueline Cortez was around. I now knew she'd moved my coffee mug. It hadn't been Harry, unfortunately. At least Caspian said she would have done something like that to be mean.

"I seem to be the only ghost who can't shake free of you," he'd said. "The kitchen antics were not light-hearted fun," he'd gone on to say. "Moving your cup would have been to see you squirm." I'd been advised to stay away from Jacqueline. "She has a mean streak," Caspian said.

But how does one stay away from a ghost? They come into your life without an invitation.

Was Jacqueline here now, plotting her next joke? Maybe this time with knives.

I continued to think about the strangeness of last night until I heard footsteps coming down the stairs. Not the lightness of Eve but someone heavier. Not as heavy as Caspian.

I blinked, hoping to lighten my vision. Still blackness. The footsteps were closer, now in the hall. I turned to face my ghost. "Who's there?" I said.

"Great Googly Mooglies," Carlos said. "You're up early."

"Still up," I said, bragging that I'd had the worst sleep of anyone, something the three of us often did. I remembered I had a bone to pick with Carlos and met him head on, conversationally. "I realize you were listening to me last night."

In the last twelve hours, so much had happened that was beyond amazing that being spied on seemed minor. Still, I had to address it.

"How did you know?"

"Just because I'm blind, you don't have the right to try to put one over on me, do you understand?"

He stopped nearby, and I could smell his Eau Sauvage. "It wasn't like that."

"It's an invasion of privacy, like if I bugged your cell phone," I said.

He moved in beside me and poured a cup of coffee. "Let's sit at the table, I'll explain."

"I hope you poured that for me. Add just a tiny bit of cream," I said and found my way to the table.

I heard Carlos texting and realized he was summoning Eve to join him. Coward. They'd have been in this together. He poured a second cup and walked slowly to the table. "We were worried you might fall down the stairs. You don't call Eve for help when we ask you to. You just navigate your way back to your room."

Two days ago, I would have been furious at them. Little did Carlos know, they were going to get off easy today because I had something bigger than being spied on in my bag of tricks. I had a ghost who appeared before me as if he was living. I had vision when he was around and had yet to tell my awesome twosome the particulars of all this amazing news.

But first, I'd make them sweat it out. Fall over themselves apologizing and vow never to do this again. I had to maintain my position as their boss, even if I was their blind boss.

Eve's footsteps padded down the hall hurriedly and she entered the kitchen. "Don't be angry, Bryn. It was my idea. I just wanted Carlos…"

"Sit down, both of you." I clutched the hot mug in my hands and waited for them.

Both Carlos and Eve were used to being told to be quiet and were really good at waiting to speak because on investigations, their silence was imperative. When I realized they were sitting at the table, waiting, I spoke my mind. "Bugging me or watching me without my knowledge, is not acceptable. Do you understand?"

"Yes." Their voices were whispers.

"I won't tolerate it again." I sounded so serious, when in truth I was bursting to tell them my big news. "This is your warning to not interfere again with either my private investigations or my personal space. When I tell you to leave me, it's just as if I was still a sighted person. You need to leave me and respect my wishes. Is that clear?"

"It is," Eve said.

I continued. "You are both my friends and my employees, and I know that's hard sometimes, but when we're on an investigation, like last night, you are only my employees and under an obligation to do as I say. Unless I ask you to do something you feel is wrong." I now understood where they were coming from. "In a case like that, you can voice your opinion but under no circumstances can you ever again bug me or spy on me, even if you feel it's in my best interest."

I took a sip of my coffee.

"Now, tell me what in the world you were thinking last night to listen in on my investigation."

"Bryn," Eve said. "It was my idea. I asked Carlos to put a bug under the table because I worried you'd get up, not call me to help you, and fall down the stairs. I just worry that you're trying to do too much too fast," she said. I heard tears in her voice. "And it turned out I was right." Her voice hitched. "You didn't call me, and I slept through the night only realizing that just now." She turned to Carlos. "You were supposed to phone me if she started downstairs!" Her voice had risen.

"I didn't even know she'd left the third floor," Carlos said, "until I heard her bedroom door close, so I'm sorry. Our plan was flawed in so many ways. And Bryn, I didn't really overhear what you were saying. I was working in the den," Carlos said, "half listening. You seemed to be talking about Rachel and I tuned out."

Although these two knew all about my relationship with my mother, I didn't really want anyone to hear my babbling last night. It was embarrassing enough to think a stranger, even a ghost, had heard me. I'd gotten on a tangent and let loose all these emotions about my life. I didn't want anyone but that cat, Moonraker, to hear my speech, but it turned out one ghost, one cat, and one employee had been privy to the fact that Rachel and I had once had the same boyfriend, at the same time, unbeknownst to either of us. That was a tidbit I kept under lock and key, especially because the thought of that boyfriend cheating on us with each other was sickening to me. Rachel had laughed when she found out, but my relationship with Justin had been much more serious. On my part only, it turned out.

Eve sniffed. She was crying. Now I felt bad I'd made her cry, the sensitive thing she was. "OK, you two," I said. "No more of this spying stuff. If I fall down the stairs and break my arm, you are not responsible. But you have to allow that I'm going to keep trying stuff to become more independent. Being blind sucks big-time, and I have to have moments when I don't rely on you."

"I understand," she sniffed.

"Get a cup of coffee, Eve, because now I have something incredible to tell you both about this pirate ghost who is not a pirate and doesn't appreciate we call him that. He's a reputable sea dog from the 1850's named Captain Caspian Cortez."

***

We had to leave Cove House that morning. The Roslyn Eatery was waiting for the follow-up to our investigation. And I had a reunion with Hodor later, something I was looking forward to with such delight, it was hard to concentrate on much else. I'd sleep with the warmth of Hodor on my bed in Floatville tonight. That was something else to look forward to.

Although I hated to walk away from this gold mine of paranormal activity, I knew we could pick up our Oregon investigation where we'd left off in a few days. We'd be back to the coast as soon as we could. I'd only mentioned I was leaving for a fortnight in an effort to bring the ghost out of hiding. We hadn't intended to be gone long at all. Certainly not two weeks.

Our original plan had been to return to the coast in a week, but things changed now that I had Caspian and because of him had my sight. I'd decided to temporarily move Moody Investigations headquarters to Oregon for the Spring. April was a few days away, the rain would let up soon, and I had an idea of how to proceed on the mystery of Caspian's murder in exchange for sight.

These next weeks I would be torn between accommodating three beings of the masculine persuasion — Caspian, Jim, and Hodor. I had obligations to each of them. I also had to accommodate my mother and her need for a place to hang her witch hat for a few weeks. I'd told Eve and Carlos, who feared her equally, that my mother would return to Oregon with us. I hadn't been able to see the look they exchanged but could imagine it involved wide eyes in fear and maybe even a retching parody from Carlos. I'd initially balked at the idea of Rachel's invasion, but she reminded me several times in one conversation that she'd provided a roof over my selfish head for years. "The least you can do for me is let me stay in your guest room for a few nights."

Living under the same roof as my mother would be challenging enough, but I said yes to two weeks. Then, it became three weeks. Every time I spoke with her the visit increased by another few days, something that made me a tiny bit suspicious. And wary.

"I want to see the house you inherited," she'd said. "I love the Oregon coast."

My friend, Rhonda, a psychologist, once advised me, "Imagine yourself in a suit of armor, not letting your mother's verbal daggers able to penetrate." In my mind, I even wore the headgear too, like a jouster, with not even my eyes showing. Even before I went blind.

While Eve and Carlos packed up any equipment we'd need for the Roslyn case, I decided to enjoy a second cup of coffee on the porch. I tapped my way outside, in time to "Great Bowls of Fire." I'd always been careful to hide my screechy singing voice, but these days, I couldn't have cared less. Being blind afforded me liberties I hadn't felt before and it was liberating.

"You shake my butt and you rattle my pain," I sang. "Goodness Graces, Great Bowls of Fire."

Finding the wicker chair, I seated myself with my mug of hot coffee and cream. Bundled in a red fiberfill parka and a wool beanie, I let Carlos and Eve do all the work loading The Marshmallow and thought about their reactions to my recent revelation.

These two were used to hearing I saw ghosts, communicated with them in some way, had feelings and twinges and visions, but they'd never heard me say I had a three-hour conversation with someone who'd been dead over a hundred years. Not until this morning. I'd told them everything. Had I been able to see Carlos and Eve, I was sure their mouths were open as I described Caspian, his way of speaking, even the fact that he called my face grotesque after all that attention Eve spent on my makeup.

"He was damp from drowning," I'd said. "He squishes slightly in his boots and wants me to find out how he died to give him a proper burial."

Eve wondered why they couldn't see him and a niggling thought wormed its way into my mind to ask myself if she believed I'd seen a ghost at all. After all, I'd lied on camera about seeing blood on the wall. Eve knew I could lie now. Convincingly.

"I don't know why you can't see him. Neither does he." I remembered a Primrose cousin having an imaginary friend when he was eight-years-old and all my weird relatives believing that he had a spirit guide who was a super-hero until he confessed his lie at the age of eighteen. Other families might have sent him for counseling. Mine praised his mojo, then when he turned out to be a fake, they simply chuckled and said he had the Primrose imagination.

The morning air was crisp enough on the porch to keep me awake. A crow called from the trees to my right and took flight. I heard the wings flap as it passed the space not far off the porch.

"Do we really need everything for Roslyn?" Eve asked.

"We do."

For the first time in months, I was almost happy. As happy as I could be at this point. My heart felt lighter, like when I'm lying in bed with an entity on top of me, unable to move and the scary thing lifts off me and dissipates. This morning, something dark and oppressive had lifted from my psyche but I wasn't sure what it was.

"I'm sorry I can't help you guys," I said as Eve walked by with a heavy box, my lips twitching in a smile.

Carlos followed. "No, you're not. You love being the pampered talent."

They both stopped in front of me.

"Do you think," Eve ventured, "Caspian will leave the house and come with you to Roslyn?"

"I know he can because I saw him at The Eatery. I'm hoping he does it again." The cawing crow took up again in a tree to my left.

"At least he isn't with you all the time, hovering," Carlos said. "That would be invasive." Carlos picked up a heavy box from the porch and started down the steps for The Marshmallow. "If he was here now, you'd be able to see us doing all the work."

"And you could help us," Eve laughed.

I looked to where Caspian had appeared, leaning against the post at the top of the stairs smiling smugly. I turned to look Eve in her beautiful black eyes and grinned, my eyebrows arched.

"What makes you think I can't see you?"

Eve shot me a look of surprise. She spun around to scan the porch, attempting to see if Caspian was present. "Is he here?" she asked.

I pointed to the man standing directly behind Eve, a man who had his arms out as if to reveal himself. He stared into her face six feet away.

"I don't see him," Eve said disappointed.

It was fricking awesome being able to see, even if my sight was sporadic and dependent on the presence of a ghost who came and went. "I guess the sea captain is just my ghost." I stared hard at the man on my porch.

Caspian's eyes sparkled in the morning light as he dipped his head as if to say, "You're welcome."

I laughed out loud. I couldn't help myself.

The End

If you enjoyed DEAD AHEAD, a review would be greatly appreciated. Reviews help other readers find good books and make this author deliriously happy.
~ Kim

To be in on giveaways and news, sign up for Kim's Monthly Newsletter here:
www.bit.ly/KimHNews

Be a part of the *Kim Hornsby Beach Club* on Facebook. Everyone welcome to join!

Novels by Kim Hornsby

<u>Dream Jumper Series</u>
The Dream Jumper's Promise – Book 1
The Dream Jumper's Secret – Book 2
The Dream Jumper's Pursuit – Book 3
Girl of his Dream - Prequel
Dream Come True – Book 4

<u>Moody & The Ghost Series</u>
Dead Ahead – Book 1
Batten Down – Book 2
Coming About – Book 3
Hoist the Jib – Book 4

Necessary Detour

About the Author

Kim Hornsby is an Amazon #1 Bestselling Author, having shared space on the top five bestseller list with J.D. Robb and Nicolas Sparks. Kim's Dream Jumper Series is optioned for film with the first movie to be THE DREAM JUMPER' PROMISE which won the Chanticleer Paranormal Mystery Thriller Award, was nominated as Best Indie First Book and was a finalist in the Rone Awards. Her screenplay for that book is a multi-award winner. Her Romantic Suspense, Necessary Detour, has reached top 5 in all Kindle Store.

In her former life, Kim taught scuba in Fiji and Hawaii, as a singer opened shows for Jay Leno and Maya Angelou, once found a boa constrictor under her bed, has taken supplies to remote Nicaraguan villages, sang on 60 Minutes, scuba dived with dolphins, whales and sharks and was the host of an international infomercial. These days she writes books outside Seattle, overlooking a tree-lined lake.

A mother of two, wife to one, messy housekeeper, dog lover and a voracious reader, Kim was born in Ontario, Canada, lived in Toronto, Vancouver, Maui, Whistler, and Taipei. Kim spends her mad money on travel and plane tickets are often found on her desk, reminding her to write bestsellers.

RECIPE ROUNDUP

HUEVOS RANCHEROS

Feeds Three Paranormal Investigators

6 eggs
3 tortillas
¼ cup salsa
¼ cup shredded Jack cheese
1 diced onion
1 can black beans, drained
1 green pepper cut in small chunks
1 clove garlic
Sour cream
½ cup sliced black olives
1 avocado sliced

Fry onion and pepper in olive oil until soft, add garlic
Scramble eggs with cheese
Warm beans and steam tortillas
Combine olives, eggs, salsa, beans, sour cream, and
avocado in a tortilla and keep the thing shut while you
eat!

*Bryn dictates the instructions to Eve, including how to
fold a tortilla beginning at the bottom and pulling in both
sides tightly.

CHICKEN SALAD

4 chicken skinless, boneless chicken breasts cooked, cut into small cubes
½ stalk of celery, chopped
½ cup of halved seedless grapes
¼ cup of almond slivers
½ cup of Hellman's mayo
½ lime – juiced
Salt and pepper to taste

Mix everything together and serve in a sandwich or in a croissant. Serve with butter lettuce.

BRYN'S EASY CHICKEN SALAD

Go to the closest Deli or Costco. Buy chicken salad
Put it in a wrap or pita pocket to keep it contained for easy eating

CLASSIC LASAGNA

1-pound lean ground beef
½ cup minced onion
2 cloves crushed garlic
1 can (28 oz) crushed tomatoes
2 6-oz cans tomato paste
2 6.5 oz cans tomato sauce

½ cup water

2 TBS white sugar

1 ½ tsp dried basil

1 tsp Italian seasoning

1 TBS salt

¼ tsp black pepper

4 TBS chopped fresh parsley

12 Lasagna noodles

16 oz. Ricotta cheese

1 egg

½ tsp salt

¾ pound sliced mozzarella cheese

¾ cup grated parmesan cheese

In a Dutch Oven cook ground beef, onion and garlic over medium heat until browned. Stir in crushed tomatoes, tomato paste, tomato sauce and water. Season with basil, sugar and Italian seasoning, 1TB salt, pepper and 2 TB parsley, Simmer covered for ½ hours, stirring every 1/2 hour.

Bring a large pot of lightly salted water to a boil. Cook lasagna noodles for 10 minutes, drain and rinse with cold water. In a mixing bowl, combine ricotta cheese with egg, parsley and ½ tsp salt.

Preheat oven to 375 degrees.

Spread meat sauce on 9 x 13 baking dish. Arrange noodles, spread ½ ricotta mix, top with 1/3 mozzarella slices. Pour 1 ½ cups meat sauce over and sprinkle with ¼ cup Parmesan. Repeat layers and top with mozzarella and parmesan.

Cover with foil sprayed with cooking spray.

Bake 25 minutes, remove foil, bake 25 more minutes, let stand for 15 minutes.

OR…

BRYN'S SUPER-EASY LASAGNA

> 2 jars of Marinara Meat Sauce
> I package of Lasagna noodles
> Lots of Mozzarella and Parmesan
> I Tub of Ricotta
> Salt, pepper and parsley

Pour ¼ of a jar of sauce in the bottom of a lasagna pan. Layer uncooked noodles, meat sauce, ricotta and mozzarella. Repeat 2 times. Season carefully. Bake at 375 for one hour with Mozzarella on top.

Made in the USA
Las Vegas, NV
05 September 2023

77092540R00089